Melbourne and Mars

MY MYSTERIOUS LIFE ON TWO PLANETS

Extracts from the Diary of a Melbourne Merchant

JOSEPH FRASER

*with an introduction by ALEXANDRA ROGINSKI
and ZACHARY KENDAL*

 **Grattan Street Press**

Grattan Street Press is the imprint of the teaching press based in the School of Culture and Communication at the University of Melbourne, Parkville, Australia.

Cover illustration, *Lantern Slide - Miniature Panorama Format Multiple Image, Astronomy* (circa 1820-1860), sourced from Museums Victoria (https://collections.museumvictoria.com.au/items/1586664).
Melbourne and Mars: My Mysterious Life on Two Planets was first published in book form in 1889.

Grattan Street Press
School of Culture and Communication
John Medley Building,
Parkville, VIC 3010
www.grattanstreetpress.com
Printed in Australia

A catalogue record for this work is available from the National Library of Australia

SERIES INTRODUCTION

The Colonial Australian Popular Fiction series brings the excitement and diversity of colonial Australian fiction to the attention of contemporary readers – and there is certainly some remarkable fiction to read here.

Encompassing both novels and short-story collections, the series will include a range of popular genres that flourished during the colonial period: the bush sketch, the Lemurian novel, crime and detective fiction, the colonial romance, the Gothic tale, the convict novel, the goldfields adventure, and the bushranger novel. Some of the authors were bestsellers in their day, and their work can still take us by surprise. We aim to make Australian Colonial fiction accessible to contemporary readers – and we hope the design and layout of these works will be helpful here.

But we also want to honour the original forms of these works. So we have reprinted from first editions or from the serialisation of a work in newspapers or journals. Each publication includes a short introduction written by academic specialists, which provides a brief biography of the author (or authors) and offers critical insight into the work and its contexts. We would be particularly pleased if some of our publications eventually became set texts in university or senior secondary courses. We believe these vibrant works from our turbulent past have much to offer all readers of Australian literature. Some of them – especially those exploring the colonial frontier – can be confronting in the intensity of their racism and the level of their violence against Aboriginal people. But it is important for contemporary Australians to experience the legacies of colonialism in all their dark complexity.

By doing so, we can begin to understand our historical condition and work towards a more reconciled future.

The Colonial Australian Popular Fiction series is an ongoing collaboration between the Grattan Street Press and the Australian Centre, both based within the School of Culture and Communication at the University of Melbourne.

Ken Gelder and Rachael Weaver

CONTENTS

INTRODUCTION

Alexandra Roginski and Zachary Kendal

When *Melbourne and Mars: My Mysterious Life on Two Planets* appeared in late 1889, Australian society buzzed with debate about Federation of the colonies and the roles that socialism, women's rights, science and religion would play in the future nation. Joseph Fraser's strange novel emerged from a literary flurry of popular utopian fiction that realised new sociological models in future or alien worlds. That summer, in the quiet suburb of Hawthorn, Fraser was also dying of consumption at the age of 46, his lungs crackling with each heaving cough. He had published pamphlets based on the popular science of phrenology, including one on how science could bring us closer to a Christian God, and another evocatively titled *Husbands: How to Select Them, How to Manage Them, How to Keep Them.*[1] But *Melbourne and Mars*, his magnum opus, arrived as a manifesto for a utopian society founded on science, socialism and altruism, veiled by a science-fictional narrative.

Fraser was born during the mid 1840s in Carlisle, in northern England's textile country. The son of a phrenologist, Fraser himself took up a career in this contested (and since discredited) science, which proposed that character and intellect could be judged from the shape of a person's head. Often remembered in our settler-colonial context as a form of racial science, phrenology's mid-nineteenth century rise in popularity stemmed also from middle-class and aspirational working-class

---

1 *Husbands* saw two editions in Melbourne: one published by A. H. Massina and Co. and another by E. W. Cole, both undated but likely from the late 1880s. See also: Joseph Fraser, *The Religion of Phrenology: Lecture* (Auckland: Wilsons & Horton, ca.1880).

concerns with personal advancement – motivations inherent to liberal thought. At the age of 31, Fraser married Annie Barron in Lancashire, and within a few years the couple departed for Aotearoa New Zealand. There they scratched a living from the vibrant lecturing circuit that often featured phrenologists, Fraser even reading the head of Māori spiritual leader Te Whiti in Taranaki in 1879, before sailing across the Tasman to the Colony of Victoria in 1885.[2]

Melbourne and Mars sprang from a colonial context of growing interest in population health and a metropolitan milieu breathless with the optimism of the New Thought movement, which historian Frank Bongiorno has described as an agglomeration of experimental ideas related to health, mind and paranormal phenomena associated with healer and Christian mystic Mary Baker Eddy.[3] Annie Fraser was herself a hydropathist (a practitioner of a therapeutic system involving bathing) and lecturer on women's health, and Joseph Fraser promoted ideas of health and an ethos of responsibility for one's self-care. Always focused on civic life, the Englishman also penned a regular column in Melbourne's *Herald* in the 1880s about prominent political figures.[4] Adopting principles developed by the United States Fowler family (founders of a phrenological empire) for scientifically based partner selection, part of the nineteenth-century concern with heredity, his lectures even featured 'experimental marriages', in which he invited a cluster of single men and women onto the stage and matched them based on the qualities of their head measurements.[5]

---

2 'Professor Fraser's Visit to Parihaka,' *Taranaki Herald*, June 7, 1879, 2.

3 Frank Bongiorno, 'A Short History of New Thought in Australia: 1890–1914,' *Australian Cultural History*, no. 23 (2004): 26.

4 Fraser's column was titled 'Pen and Ink Sketches of Prominent Persons.'

5 'Professor Fraser's Lecture,' *Warragul Guardian*, May 14, 1885, 3.

Neither children nor health blessed the Frasers. When the phrenologist declared insolvency in September 1889, he claimed a sickness of four years' duration, his assets limited to valueless shares in real estate, the illustrations and charts with which he lectured, as well as furniture, an American organ, and a watch and chain. Fraser died just weeks after the publication of *Melbourne and Mars*, in the early days of 1890. Yet his novel leaves an imprint of his dreams for a different life, a lens through which to stargaze at a mélange of ideas about socialism, the environment, childrearing, scientific progress and Australia's federated future.

Melbourne and Mars tells the story of an unassuming colonial merchant who begins living a second life in a Martian utopia. The conceit is that Fraser has merely edited this merchant's diary, occasionally inserting his own commentary, and referring to the merchant narrator pseudonymously as Adam Jacobs to protect his identity. Jacobs's diary records an extraordinary double life: by a division of the soul, he also has a younger alter-ego, Charles Frankston, on Mars. Although much of Mars resembles Colonial Melbourne, the 'Martials' are smaller, more beautiful, and thrive in an altruistic socialist utopia of abundance and technological marvels. We glimpse phrenology and physiognomy guiding crucial judgments of character, such as when Jacobs is introduced by Fraser as having 'a finely formed head' that is 'narrow at the bottom, wide at the top, and ... has not much brain in the region of selfish propensities, ... [while] his moral brain is high and wide'.[6]

A political philosophy of altruistic socialism scaffolds Fraser's Martian utopia. This democratic socialist model does not acknowledge class struggle and functions through a common

6 *Melbourne and Mars*, 5.

sense of morality rather than state controls. On Mars, a central government apportions employment, food and material goods to citizens. Crime is unknown. Yet this is not the socialism of *The Communist Manifesto*, and Tod Moore notes that *Melbourne and Mars* 'appears to be indebted more to Edward Bellamy than to Karl Marx'.[7] Indeed, American author Bellamy's highly influential utopian novel *Looking Backward 2000–1887*, published in Boston in 1888, shares commonalities with *Melbourne and Mars*, although it is uncertain whether Fraser had access to a copy while writing his novel.[8] More direct Australian responses to *Looking Backward* would emerge in the 1890s, including David A. Andrade's *The Melbourne Riots and How Harry Holdfast and His Friends Emancipated the Workers* (Melbourne: Andrade & Co., 1892) and Samuel Albert Rosa's *The Coming Terror; or, The Australian Revolution* (Sydney: S. A. Rosa, 1894), both of which challenge the slow and peaceful transitions to socialism envisaged by Bellamy and Fraser.

In its moral exhortations, Fraser's model is best characterised as 'ethical socialism' or even 'Christian socialism', movements that allied political virtue with altruism and self-development. And religion flourishes in Fraser's utopia, with the Martials practising a kind of non-conformist Christianity (referred to as 'a pure Theism') that swells during tabernacle-style services in worship of a deity of dual male and female form.[9] In their emphasis on moral development and uplifting humanism, such models of socialism did not argue for structural reform

---

7 Tod Moore, 'Melbourne and Mars: The Australian All Electric Communist Utopia,' *Labour History*, no. 87 (2004): 209.

8 Moore suggests that Fraser may have had access to an early copy of *Looking Backward*, although it was not published for a popular readership until 1889, and it is difficult to determine when the book made it to the Australian colonies. Moore, 'Melbourne and Mars,' 216.

9 *Melbourne and Mars*, 167.

or revolution and could nestle alongside bourgeois social organisation.[10]

Despite its socialism, *Melbourne and Mars* subtly promotes a model for class society. For example, travellers on Mars reside at particular hostels based on their occupations, not because they are different but, somewhat tenuously, because people 'prefer to associate with their companions in labour'.[11] As one mentor to Frankston expounds, 'We are all altruistic socialists, all democrats; all either as individuals or as classes willing to waive our own rights in favour of others, and yet we cannot be equal'.[12] The book therefore reveals a preoccupation with refuting a common critique of socialism: that it would produce mediocrity. In the 'perfect socialism' of Mars, 'No class can prey upon any other class in social life; … we cannot be equal in power and capacity, hence some are greater than others'.[13] Intellect and virtue on Mars derive in part from a Victorian ethic of self-cultivation.

The novel presents a bold technological optimism: science guides life on the Red Planet. *Melbourne and Mars* emerged during a golden age of literature that considered how science and technology might aid social organisation, a period that Nan Bowman Albinski describes as spanning the 1880s and 1890s.[14] A story of technological progress, it reveals Fraser's fascination with electricity, which dominated technological transformation during the late nineteenth century. On Mars, electricity is free

10 Frank Bongiorno, 'Love and Friendship: Ethical Socialism in Britain and Australia,' *Australian Historical Studies* 32, no. 116 (2001): 4; Renate Howe, 'Protestantism, Social Christianity and the Ecology of Melbourne, 1890–1900,' *Historical Studies* 19, no. 74 (1980): 65–66.

11 *Melbourne and Mars*, 134.

12 *Melbourne and Mars*, 134.

13 *Melbourne and Mars*, 143.

14 Nan Bowman Albinski, 'A Survey of Australian Utopian and Dystopian Fiction,' *Australian Literary Studies* 13, no. 1 (1987): 16.

and limitless, with the Martials having abandoned fossil fuels for an endless supply of energy tapped from deep underground. One reviewer, who recognised the book as part of a genre, drew parallels with Edward Bulwer-Lytton's *The Coming Race*, an 1871 novel that told of a majestic people living within the earth's core who had uncovered an endless source of energy (known as 'Vril').[15] Everything on Mars is strictly and scientifically ordered and the book brims with straight lines – electrical lines, train lines, the lines of latitude and longitude, and a snow line melted and tamed for agriculture. Technological innovations such as the zooming 'flying fish' abound, and Franklin's big break comes when he invents a method for harnessing electricity to improve crop production.

Contemporary readers may recognise the novel's concern with how to manage resources to sustain ever more humans – a debate that gathered steam from the end of the eighteenth century. *Melbourne and Mars* explicitly lambasts the ideas of political economist Robert Thomas Malthus (1766–1834), who argued that finite resources meant that a densely populated planet could not house universally happy humans.[16] In the novel, Malthus is the progenitor of a category of thinkers that Fraser derides as the gloomy 'Croakers'. The perfected state of Martial humans, according to Fraser, stems from both social organisation and natural selection – an entanglement of biological and sociological ideas common to the period – with any curtailing of population growth coming not through the misery of war,

---

15 Patrick Parrinder, *Utopian Literature and Science: From the Scientific Revolution to Brave New World and Beyond* (New York: Palgrave Macmillan, 2015), 82–86; Edward Bulwer-Lytton, *The Coming Race*, ed. David Seed, (Middletown, CT: Wesleyan University Press, 2005), xlii.

16 Thomas Malthus, *An Essay on the Principle of Population* (London: J Johnson, 1798).

disease, or famine, but through altruism and human ingenuity. And readers familiar with ecological arguments for veganism will recognise the Martial observation of the wastefulness of raising beasts in captivity because of the vast quantities of grain required as feed. Yet the novel's late-nineteenth-century sensibilities shine through, not least in passages where characters celebrate the extermination of dangerous animals and the regimentation of landscape, both at odds with our modern reverence for wilderness. Fraser argues against livestock cultivation, but does not espouse vegetarianism, as many progressives of the time did: Martials eat fish and hold animal life in lower value, because 'a human life … [is] capable of more happiness'.[17]

Fraser's work also reflects the Martian moment in popular science and literature, which drew momentum from the erroneous observations in 1877 by Italian astronomer Giovanni Schiaparelli of 'canals' on Mars, soon interpreted as irrigation systems. In *Melbourne and Mars*, Frankston in fact narrates that Earth's astronomers had 'found a long, straight line on Mars, something that indicated human handiwork'.[18] Although other planets in our galaxy had inspired utopian works from at least the early seventeenth century, Schiaparelli's 'canals' became evidence of intelligent life and inspired works such as H. G. Wells's *The War of the Worlds* (1897) and Bellamy's *The Blindman's World* (1886) before being debunked in 1909.

With the women's suffrage movement in full sway by the late-nineteenth century, many Australian utopians addressed the issue of women's rights. Decidedly negative positions feature in the deeply conservative Christian utopia *The Great Statesman: A Few Leaves From the History of Antipodea, Anno Domini 3000* by

---

17 *Melbourne and Mars*, 107.
18 *Melbourne and Mars*, 130.

'Can C' (Sydney: Edward Lee, 1885)[19] and in Millie Finkelstein's satirical anti-utopia *The Newest Woman: The Destined Monarch of the World* (Melbourne: Pat Finn, 1895). Suffragettes, however, produced their own utopian visions; these included Henrietta Augusta Dugdale's *A Few Hours in a Far-Off Age* (Melbourne: McCarron, Bird & Co., 1883), Catherine Helen Spence's *A Week in the Future* (serialised in *The Centennial Magazine*, December 1888 to July 1889) and Mary Ann Moore-Bentley's *A Woman of Mars; or, Australia's Enfranchised Woman* (Sydney: Edwards, Dunlop & Co., 1901). Fraser seemingly sympathised with the women's rights movement and perhaps drew inspiration from Dugdale and Spence. On Mars, women and men enjoy equality and companionate partnerships, and women are represented in political, medical, and academic positions. As Frankston narrates toward the end of the novel: 'Women and men are free and equal; a woman does not resign her name or any social right'.[20]

Melbourne and Mars also reflects a surge in support for the idea of a united Australia, which the historian John Hirst notes as manifesting in a 'festival of poetry' that by the 1870s celebrated Federation as divine destiny.[21] In *Melbourne and Mars*, one finds an advocacy for worldwide federation akin to that championed by E. W. Cole (1832–1918), proprietor of Cole's Book Arcade in Melbourne. In 1886, Cole wrote and published a pamphlet on the federation of the world, setting out a utopian vision for a peaceful and prosperous planet. Cole's utopia embraced flying machines and other advanced technologies,

19 Sargent attributes authorship of *The Great Statesman* to Joseph Broadbent
   Holmes. Lyman Tower Sargent, 'Australian Utopian Literature: An
   Annotated, Chronological Bibliography 1667–1999,' *Reason in Revolt* (2009),
   http://www.reasoninrevolt.net.au/bib/PR0001745.htm.

20 *Melbourne and Mars*, 166.

21 John Hirst, *The Sentimental Nation* (South Melbourne: Oxford University
   Press, 2000), 15.

wealth redistribution and universal suffrage, and a common language and religion to unite the masses.[22] *Melbourne and Mars* explores these ideals of federation, which likely contributed to Cole's decision to publish the novel. On Fraser's Mars, a 'Grand Federal Government', established after a 'declaration of Eternal Peace', manages the harsh planet for the bounty of all. As a mentor scientist tells Frankston after showing him the wonders of the Martial capital, 'Had we not united in some such way these great [civic] works could not have been undertaken'.[23] Later, a doctor tells Frankston that 'the race on earth is young yet, it is that of a child. … Arbitration between nations is but commencing, and Federation of a few of the most civilised and powerful nations is but a dream of the future.'[24]

The Federation of Mars, however, seems less grand if we consider its homogeneity. Fraser's ideal society was not explicitly structured around the xenophobic ideologies found elsewhere in colonial Australian fiction and works from the early decades post-Federation.[25] But the ideal society that he builds is distinctly Anglo Saxon, and the narrative is notable for almost entirely lacking any characters of colour, and none that function as more than a swift plot device. In the ideal society on Mars, all the Martials are white and bear Anglo Saxon names, as do major landmarks. When taken as a template for a utopian Australia, it

---

22 'The Federation of the World Inevitable Before the Year 2000' was later bound into the back of Cole's *Fun Doctor* (Melbourne: E. W. Cole, [1886]). Cole's Book Arcade also produced a series of collectible medals promoting worldwide federation in the mid-1880s and ran an essay-writing competition on the topic in 1890. Cole Turnley, *Cole of the Book Arcade: A Biography of E. W. Cole* (Hawthorn, Vic: Cole Publications, 1974), 84, 102–103.

23 *Melbourne and Mars*, 101.

24 *Melbourne and Mars*, 109.

25 Albinski, 'Survey,' 19.

leaves no place for Indigenous Australians or non-white people – consistent with racial prejudices of the period.[26]

The reception of *Melbourne and Mars* is difficult to gauge without data on sales and readerships, but the scarcity of newspaper reviews suggest that it did not blaze through public life. Fraser's early death on 7 January 1890 no doubt stymied efforts to promote the work.[27] While a reviewer in *The Herald* argued that 'no one who reads the first half-dozen pages is likely to put the book down until the last sentence is reached,' another scribbling in the *Weekly Times* sighed that the book 'results in our making the acquaintance of some Martial politicians duller and more prolix than their kind among the earth-born.'[28] Yet, despite its often-didactic tone, the novel contains episodes of adventure and character development that most nineteenth-century utopian novels lack, including Bellamy's *Looking Backward. Melbourne and Mars* remains, as Russell Blackford, Van Ikin and Sean McMullen note in their history of Australian science fiction, 'one of the most important Australian utopian novels.'[29]

In his fading months, Fraser might have perused reports of the fledgling mission of politician Henry Parkes for the Federation of the Australian colonies, but he never had the chance to see whether the new nation could at all progress towards a unified likeness

26 Cole's vision of a federated world was also racist and homogenous, with the author stipulating that in his ideal future, 'all savage and barbarous races will be subjugated by more advanced nations, civilised, and then, like grown-up children, allowed the rights of equals.' Quoted in Turnley, *Cole*, 84.

27 Joseph Fraser Death Certificate, 2347/1890, Victorian Registry of Births Deaths and Marriages.

28 'Review: Melbourne and Mars,' *The Herald* (Melbourne), November 26, 1889, 3; 'Melbourne and Mars,' *Weekly Times* (Melbourne), December 7, 1889, 7.

29 Russell Blackford, Van Ikin and Sean McMullen, *Strange Constellations: A History of Australian Science Fiction* (Westport, CT: Greenwood Press, 1999), 26.

of Mars.[30] Deprived of a future himself, his imagination carried him into a society thousands of years more advanced than the scarcity endured in dreary Melbourne. His utopia was arguably deeply personal, as similarities between names suggest (Jacobs/Joseph, Frankston/Fraser). The biography of the book's earthly protagonist, Adam Jacobs, also yields many similarities to Fraser's own life: Jacobs emigrates to Australia from the same northern part of England in which Fraser was born, and he begins his interplanetary adventures at 45, almost exactly the age at which Fraser wrote the novel. In *Melbourne and Mars*, Fraser presented a perfect society where scientific achievement by curious dreamers received its due. In real life, Fraser's optimistic social science could not save him from insolvency or the hungry bacterium in his lungs. But at least he could write Charles Frankston, a Martial protagonist who met with sweet rewards – a 'Freedom Badge' and a valorised role in the development of an ideal world.

ALEXANDRA ROGINSKI is a research fellow with the Alfred Deakin Institute for Citizenship and Globalisation at Deakin University whose work spans fields including the history of science and cultural heritage. She completed her PhD on the history of popular phrenology in Australia and Aotearoa New Zealand through the ANU School of History in 2018. She is the author of *The Hanged Man and the Body Thief: Finding Lives in a Museum Mystery* (Monash University Publishing, 2015).

ZACHARY KENDAL is a librarian at Deakin University. His PhD research in Literary and Cultural Studies at Monash University examined ethics and science fiction. He is also an editor of *Ethical Futures and Global Science Fiction* with Aisling Smith, Giulia Champion and Andrew Milner (Palgrave Macmillan, 2020).

---

30 Hirst, *Sentimental Nation*, 1.

WORKS CITED

Albinski, Nan Bowman. 'A Survey of Australian Utopian and Dystopian Fiction.' *Australian Literary Studies* 13, no. 1 (1987): 15–28.

Blackford, Russell, Van Ikin and Sean McMullen. *Strange Constellations: A History of Australian Science Fiction*. Westport, CT: Greenwood Press, 1999.

Bongiorno, Frank. 'Love and Friendship: Ethical Socialism in Britain and Australia.' *Australian Historical Studies* 32, no. 116 (2001): 1–19.

Bongiorno, Frank. 'A Short History of New Thought in Australia: 1890–1914.' *Australian Cultural History*, no. 23 (2004): 25–42.

Hirst, John. *The Sentimental Nation*. South Melbourne: Oxford University Press, 2000.

Howe, Renate. 'Protestantism, Social Christianity and the Ecology of Melbourne, 1890–1900.' *Historical Studies* 19, no. 74 (1980): 59–73.

Malthus, Thomas. *An Essay on the Principle of Population*. London: J Johnson, 1798.

Moore, Tod. 'Melbourne and Mars: The Australian All Electric Communist Utopia.' *Labour History*, no. 87 (2004): 209–220.

Parrinder, Patrick. *Utopian Literature and Science: From the Scientific Revolution to Brave New World and Beyond*. New York: Palgrave Macmillan, 2015.

Sargent, Lyman Tower. 'Australian Utopian Literature: An Annotated, Chronological Bibliography 1667–1999.' *Reason in Revolt* (2009). http://www.reasoninrevolt.net.au/bib/PR0001745.htm.

Seed, David. Introduction to *The Coming Race*, by Edward Bulwer-Lytton. Middletown, CT: Wesleyan University Press, 2005.

Turnley, Cole. *Cole of the Book Arcade: A Biography of E. W. Cole*. Hawthorn, Vic: Cole Publications, 1974.

A NOTE ON THE TEXT

Joseph Fraser's *Melbourne and Mars* was published in Melbourne in late 1889 and saw two imprints: one listing only the printers, Pater & Knapton, and another with E. W. Cole, Book Arcade, as the publisher. The source text for this volume is the copy held at the National Library of Australia, which has the Cole cover (albeit with some characters misprinted) and the original Pater & Knapton title page. The only differences between the printings are the publication details provided on the cover and title page, although the Cole version lacks the date provided by the Pater & Knapton version. Both imprints also carry the same advertisements at the back of the volume, most of which are for the author's previous publications and his phrenological services. The editors have made minor corrections to spelling, grammar and punctuation, which were idiosyncratic in the original.

Melbourne and Mars

MY MYSTERIOUS LIFE ON TWO PLANETS

INTRODUCTION

By the Editor

Some time ago, an elderly gentleman, a colonial of repute, brought to me his diaries and wished me to put them in connected form for printing. My time was too fully occupied and my health too precarious to allow me to undertake the task. However, he brought his documents and gave me unlimited time, and in some six months my co-worker was able to give him his book, written ready for the press. It was printed for private circulation only and read with avidity by those who received copies.

Some time afterwards, this gentleman mentioned a friend of his who had had some strange experiences, and recorded them in a diary for a number of years, and would like to have them put into shape for publication. I refused to undertake the task, for my professional practice was heavier than before, and I was gradually preparing some publications of my own for the press.

In spite of my refusal, there came one day by express a bundle of books of various sizes and shapes. Amongst them a day book, a ledger, a betting book, a pocket memo-randum book, two closely written diaries for certain years and a large bundle of manuscript in which an attempt had been made to put the experiences of over fifty years into a connected and readable shape. The manuscript had been offered to a Melbourne publishing firm and refused on the ground that it had neither beginning nor end, neither paragraphs nor chapters; that it was entirely unreadable and not likely to prove of interest to anyone.

Nevertheless, I straightened out the curly, crumpled, dirty, dog-eared sheets and laid them under the heaviest thing in my office – a box of electrotypes and zincotypes used in illustrating various publications. After they had been here a couple of weeks and got flattened, I took them up one day when I did not feel fit for heavier work and began to turn them over, glancing at their contents here and there. It was not long before I saw that this diarist was either a monomaniac, a dreamer, or a man who had undergone a series of the strangest experiences that ever fell to the lot of man, and that in any case, his story, if told, would be sure to attract more than mere local attention. For twenty-five years, the man had either been living a dual life, spending his time upon two planets of our solar system, or he had been dreaming half his time one of the most vivid and consecutive dreams ever recorded.

My interest was now fully aroused. I read all his musty diaries in their cramped handwriting and peculiar phrase-ology with avidity, and determined to make a careful study of the man and to see him on several occasions in order to find out his mental condition, at the same time fully intending to work up his story, no matter whether he had dreamt it or experienced it. I made an appointment with him for an evening after business hours and saw him on several occasions, while condensing his diaries and preparing a rough draft of his story.

He is more than seventy years of age, is of medium stature, has a finely formed head and a remarkably intelligent face. I liked him from the first. His appearance, though not striking, told of a thoughtful and truthful nature. He is not a pushing and enterprising man, not one who could make money; although he has had his chances, and has at times managed to get a couple of hundreds of pounds saved up for old age or a rainy day. The face is narrow at the bottom, wide at the top; and the brain is much more fully developed in the upper than the lower stories.

He has not much brain in the region of the selfish propensities and has not much capacity for the management of financial matters. Self-esteem is decidedly weak and he has not sufficient firmness to take a decided stand and resist aggression. His moral brain is high and wide; he is full of charitable and kindly feeling; he is also religious in the broadest, best and most philosophical sense of the term. His affections are deep, strong and pure, like those of a good woman, and his integrity is beyond suspicion. For the last few years, he has been employed in a subordinate capacity by a commercial firm. What little hair he has is very fine and of the silvery whiteness that tells of purity of life. His bones are fine, his skull thin, and his hands and ears thin and well formed. There is nothing fleshy, heavy or coarse about his structure. He is one of nature's gentlemen.

Ideality, sublimity, spirituality and hope are all large, but he has not much language to express his ideas either in speech or written forms. Such men are philosophical, thoughtful, dreamy, dutiful, harmless. Never pushing nor ostentatious, they do not come to the front in money-grubbing and other pursuits of a like nature. They are frequently tossed aside and do not gain the respect of the multitude. Many traits of his character come out in his story.

From first to last, I saw no trace of insanity or mono-mania. He is cheerful, happy, content and in no sense fanatical. His story will in part account for his cheerful view of life. He gave me his manuscript and all the verbal explanation necessary in the most generous manner, seeming to care more for having his experiences brought under public notice than for any possible emoluments that might result from their publication. Indeed, I had to threaten to give up all idea of making use of his strange experiences before he could be induced to take any share of financial proceeds. He would have been content to take a few copies of his book for presentation to his limited circle of friends as a sole reward for his twenty-five years of work in providing materials for the strangest story ever told by mortal man.

He has now to receive half the nett proceeds of sales so long as he requires them, as stated in the rough and ready agreement signed by the narrator and editor.

[AGREEMENT]

I, Adam Jacobs, do hereby agree to hand over for publication all my diaries to Joseph Fraser that he may put them into the form of a book, and call such book by a name that will convey some idea of its substance, the said book to be published and sold in any or all parts of the English-speaking world, and copyrighted wherever published. The book shall be sold at what may be deemed by writer and publisher a reasonable price for popular sale. I, on my part, will not put my diaries or any part of them into the hands of any other writer, nor give to any other any personal experiences, and on his part paying me half the nett proceeds of sales at the end of each six months from the date of publication.

(SIGNED) ADAM JACOBS
JOSEPH FRASER

It is not necessary to say that the real name of the diarist is not Adam Jacobs. I am not even allowed to say whether he is a Jew or a Gentile, or to give any clue to his identity. He wants his narrative to be made public, but has a horror of personal fame or notoriety.

I have decided to let the man speak in the first person whenever what he says relates his own experiences, and to let the order of the narrative be as natural and sequential as possible. But as the experiences of years will sometimes be related in as many pages, and as the material of the diaries will have to be reduced quite nine-tenths to make a handy and readable book, the language will be almost entirely my own.

CHAPTER I

AUTOBIOGRAPHICAL

'I MIGHT WRITE a volume on the details of my early and middle life, and many of my experiences would doubtless be interesting to readers in the Australian Colonies, but my experiences during the first forty-four years of my life, though stirring and eventful enough, were common to most men. Indeed there are men whom I see whenever I go to Melbourne, who have gone through more than I have in the stirring time of the gold discovery.

'I was born in the year 1818 in the then-small town of Blackburn in Lancashire. My parents were hand-loom weavers and by close attention to work on all days but St Monday they managed to make a fair living. Power-loom weaving at that time had not reduced the rates of payment and taken the work out of the hands of weavers, as it did a few years later. My mother was a hearty, merry, affectionate woman; she had received more than the ordinary education of her class, her father having been a shopkeeper and able to send his daughters, my mother and aunt, to a boarding school for a few years.

'Her marriage with my father had not been approved of by her family, but a happier marriage could scarcely have been made. My father was a thoughtful man, but his education had been neglected; he could read his Bible but even that accomplishment had been taught him by Mother. He was a very sober and industrious man and entirely devoted to his work, his little garden and his family. I was the third child of a family of five. The next younger than I was a brother, the rest were sisters.

'Mother had some of the instincts of a lady and had furnished a small front room as a parlour. On one of the walls was hung a large sampler in a glass frame – a mixture of queer pictures, as devoid of perspective as any work of Japanese art, and some Scripture texts worked in silk that had at one time been bright in colour. On a side table stood a kind of museum in glass, collected and constructed by Father, and over a cabinet in the corner was a small hanging bookcase. Of course there was the inevitable chest of drawers, and the centre table, and a bit of carpet or drugget on the floor, and sundry china ornaments on the mantelpiece and drawers.

'Mother always took us into this room on Sunday afternoon and gave us a reading lesson, and generally led us in singing a hymn, taking care that we became letter perfect in words, time and at least the air of the tune. On other days this room was sacred, except when some visitor or aunt came, when we were straightened up, put on our best behaviour and shewn in one at a time.

'Our garden was a small piece of rich land rented from a farmer nearby and shared by a neighbour of ours. We grew peas, radishes, onions, lettuce, celery, cauliflowers and cabbages, and sometimes had some to sell. Our life was a very happy one. We were poor, true, but we had plenty of food and were warmly clad. In the season we gathered whinberries, blackberries and nuts, and spent plenty of time in the open air, sometimes going miles into the country from our home in the outskirts of the town. At this time much of the spinning was done by the "Jenny", worked by hand, and my elder sisters had much of their time employed in spinning and winding cops.

'We were all taught to read and write, and reckon. Mother doing part of the teaching and Mary Carter the other part. Mrs Carter used an old weaving shop as a school, where she taught about sixty or seventy children the rudiments. So far as it went, our education was better than is generally credited to the time. Parents who thought anything of themselves took care the three Rs were well taught. Dunces were not forced to learn and pass a certain standard; when it was found out that they could not or would not learn, children were made of use by being sent to work while those who desired to learn more got a reasonable education and some became scholars.

'Indeed, I believe quite as many real scholars were turned out under the free system as under the compulsory one, and certainly workers grew up under the old mode. I was regarded as rather delicate for I made the most of my croup, measles, whooping cough, scarlatina and other diseases of childhood.

'Being the eldest boy, however, I had to do a little light work about the house – to help with the crops, to weed the garden, to run errands – and so gradually became a hardy little chap and was saved from the interesting, precocious, semi-invalidism into which so many children are now permitted to drop in these days of luxury. There are thousands of thin-necked, flat-chested, big-browed boys in this much-loved colonial land, who would soon become robust if trained as I was. My dear mother saw what was best and while taking all care of me, never gave me the impression that I was an object of special attention.

'So passed my life until my tenth year when there were serious reductions in the prices paid to hand-loom weavers. There were now over one hundred thousand power-looms in Lancashire, and although hand-looms still outnumbered them two to one, prices were reduced. John Drylands, who employed all the people about where we lived, kept reducing wages until we had to work for St Monday one-third less and began to feel the pinch of poverty.

'Mother always kept a bit of money by her for a rainy day when we were comparatively well off; but a time came when all was spent and we had only bread, dripping, porridge, and skim milk, and a few vegetables to live upon; meat and butter, eggs and cheese we seldom saw, and as a result we became weaker and lower in health, and lived dull and hopeless lives. Our faces grew pale and our clothing shabby, and when we tried to sing on Sunday afternoons our voices almost cried.

'Power-loom weavers earned more than we did and so it was decided that we should go to the mill. My two sisters went to weaving, and I and my brother to spinning. We worked from five in the morning to seven at night and had to snatch our meals. The four of us earned a little more than a pound a week. This enabled us to live more liberally, or would have done if we had had time to eat and enjoy life. Our lives were all work and sleep, and we had much unkind treatment from our employers. Father seemed to undergo a change. His garden did not interest him. We seemed to have fallen upon lawless times. Our garden beds were pillaged when there was anything worth taking, and hard times and poverty made men mad. Bread was dear, wages were low, and all the people were quarrelsome and unhappy. The air was full of storm; men gathered at street corners and in pothouses, and talked excitedly about politics and the price of corn.

'Father spent some of his time this way and got mixed up with a lot of men whom he would have cared little to meet a few years before. Poverty works such changes. These men were ground down on all hands by the action of laws that they neither made nor sanctioned, and being ignorant they became the prey of demagogues who put their one-sided statements before them. The result was the production of a crop of men ready for any crime and especially for acts of personal violence.

'About this time an election took place. Party feeling ran high. Men wore the colours of their candidates consp-icuously displayed and street fights became very com-mon. In these, several men were severely injured and some were killed outright. For the election day, special constables were sworn in and a body of troops were sent for and held in readiness. The mills were stopped, the shops closed. The polling booths were a constant scene of riot, disorder and sometimes bloodshed. Mother kept us at home all day and tried to persuade Father to stay at home too, but he went to record his vote in Penny Street in the afternoon, promising to come back before tea and tell us the news. Teatime came, but no Father; bedtime, and still no Father. Knowing that we had to be at work at five o'clock next morning, Mother sent us to bed and waited up alone – waited till the day broke and until we had gone to work. It was the first time that Father had spent a night away from home and he was never to spend another night there.

'At a little before the time for closing the poll, Father was coming out of the booth, having recorded his vote, when a wagon load of Tory voters, noisily drunk and carrying blue ribbons and rosettes, drove up to the door. There were some score of men who had been shepherded at a jerry shop – a low alehouse – all day, and who were now coming to give their votes or sell them for about ten shillings each. A lot of Darron Punsers[1] came with them to clear the way into the booth. As they jumped and tumbled out of the wagon into the crowd, they were seized on all hands by the wearers of pink and green, and a free fight commenced. The police and special constables were not equal to the occasion, and before help arrived several men were severely injured, one killed outright, and another so much hurt that he died a day or two after.

'Father was in the midst of the crowd and received a number of blows and doubtless gave as good as he got. One eye was blackened, a cut on the forehead covered his face with blood, and he received several bruises from the clog toes of a Darron Punser, kicker with the feet. Before he could get clear of his entanglement a squad of infantry charged down Penny Street and Father suffered further

---

1 'Darron' most likely refers to the industrial Lancashire town of 'Darwen', pronounced 'Darren' by locals and long known as 'Dirty Darren'. The latter word in this phrase derives from 'punce' – 'to kick' in Lancashire dialect. These 'Darron Punsers' are therefore ruffians from Darwen. See: John Nodal and George Milner, *A Glossary of the Lancashire Dialect* (London: Trübner & Co, 1875), 219; Paul Laxton, *Darwen Born, Blackburn Bred: Growing up in the Age of Affluence*, (London: New Generation, 2016).

maltreatment, and as he got up, after being rolled over and trampled upon, a constable slipped a pair of handcuffs on him and took him to the watchhouse.

'Here early next morning Mother found him, but she could not obtain his release, for he was one who had been seen struggling within a yard of where a man had fallen dead. For three weeks several men who had been arrested in that crowd were examined and remanded, and at last sent for trial to the Assize Court. Father's friends rallied around him. They testified to his general good character and conduct, and would doubtless have obtained his acquittance but for a persistent special constable, who swore that he saw Father knock the man down who had been carried dead off the street.

'The jury brought in a verdict of guilty of manslaughter, and five men were sentenced to fourteen years' transportation.

'Our tears and prayers were all of no avail. Our father, whom we had always known as a kind man, and little likely to injure anyone, was taken from us, and all we could get to know was his ultimate destination – Botany Bay.

'The first thing Mother did was to determine to go out to him and to take us with her. Aunt and Uncle were opposed to this step, but eventually they agreed and helped with the preparations and found means. Nearly a year after Father went out in a Government ship, we set sail in a barque, the Mary Jane, for Port Jackson. There were several families in the steerage with us. Two wives were going to join convicted husbands. One of the husbands had killed a hare and fought a keeper, and the other, driven by poverty and hunger, had stolen half a sheep. This was the justice of the time.

'A voyage of one hundred and fifty-two days brought us to Port Jackson. I was twelve years old when we landed.

There were four of us. Mother had been persuaded to let my younger brother and sister remain at least for a few years. She was rather sorry for this, for my sisters, about fourteen and sixteen years of age respectively, got situations immediately and I got temporary employment in a store. This left Mother at liberty to follow Father up-country, where he had been hired out by the system then in vogue.

'Mother was not long in completing her preparations. Her intention was to get work in the same neighbourhood as Father, possibly on the same station, so that she might be near him and help him to work into a condition of relative freedom as many convicts had done. Indeed, some wives had managed to get their husbands assigned to them as servants and were getting on well in business.

'Father had been assigned to a squatter some one hundred and twenty miles inland. There were no roads and no regular means of conveyance. Those who travelled at this time generally walked and carried their swag. Some rode, but horses were scarce and very high priced. Mother could not buy nor hire a horse, nor could she have ridden had there been a horse available, and a walk of one hundred and twenty miles across a trackless country was not to be thought of.

'Bullock drays went up now and then, performing the journey in a week or ten days, according to the state of the country. No other mode of travel being available, my mother secured a passage on one of these.'

CHAPTER II

MOTHER'S JOURNEY

'EARLY ONE MORNING my two sisters and I had the painful experience of parting with our dear mother. We carried her trunk to a store in George Street, where a clumsy broad-wheeled dray stood laden with flour, tea, sugar and other merchandise. The driver found a place for her amongst bags and boxes, where she might sit or even lie in tolerable comfort. The bullocks were attached, kisses were exchanged, tears freely shed by all of us, until the driver cut a painful scene short by a crack of his long whip and some mystic words that the bullocks evidently understood, though we did not. Need I say that I followed that dray several miles, that I hugged Mother till she must have been weary, and that with lingering feet and tear-dimmed eyes I walked back to Sydney too late for any work that day.

'Four uneventful days passed after Mother's departure. Sydney was at that time a very sleepy little town. The various movements of a few semi-military men, the changes amongst convicts, and the arrival and departure of a ship; these were events. On the fifth day a mail boat arrived, bringing with it a FREE PARDON for my father.

'For six weary days the bullock dray toiled on with its freight. Six days of heat and dust and thirst, of the monotonous cracking of the whip and the vigorous, but mostly unintelligible, language of the driver and his mate. Six nights of camping out and roughing it, and now the seventh day's journey, the last, has begun. Each day Mother commenced by walking a few miles. If she had known the way she would have walked on this last day and left the dray to follow. As it was she was a good mile ahead when the dray was overtaken by a mounted trooper, who asked for Mrs Jacobs. Pointing to a speck in the distance before them the driver said, "That's her."

'In a few minutes the trooper had ridden up and told my mother his errand. Told it all too abruptly, for when the full significance of his words reached her consciousness she reeled, and would have fallen, as if stricken with a blow, had not the trooper caught her and laid her gently down. There was no water at hand, but the trooper rubbed her hands, fanned her face, and forced a little whisky from a pocket flask between her lips and brought her back to life.

'By the time the dray got up to them the trooper had shown his important document and explained to Mother that he had been sent as messenger owing to the exertions of some of her friends in Sydney, else the pardon would not have reached her husband for many days yet.

'Mother pleaded with the trooper to let her be the bearer of the pardon. To this he consented, although it was not quite in accordance with his instructions and was the means of causing suffering to both my parents. Only about twelve miles remained. Mother walked that, the trooper walking by her side leading his horse. The station was reached late in the afternoon, but the squatter and his foreman and all the men were away, and the place was in charge of some native women called jins[2] and a female convict, a respectable looking woman, Mrs Finn.

'Mother and the trooper were supplied with a rough and ready kind of meal, Mrs Finn meanwhile telling how difficult it was for free people to obtain work owing to convict labour and that of the blacks. Mrs Finn could tell nothing about the convict Jacobs except that he came to the station once a fortnight for rations, and that he was trusted with an important duty on a distant part of the run. There was nothing for it but to await the return of the squatter. It was late when Mr Beedham, the squatter, returned, and later still before he would pay any attention to my mother's errand. However, when he saw the pardon releasing Jacobs from his control he expressed surprise and consternation, for that very afternoon he had found that Jacobs and his mate had been fighting at one of the huts about a jin, that he could not get to know which was in the wrong, and had sent both to a Justice of the Peace, who resided twenty miles away.

'The trooper explained to Mother that no man was allowed to inflict punishment upon his own assigned convict servant, that he was bound to have him punished by order of a magistrate or to send him back to the stockade for punishment. The squatters got over this by getting

---

2   More commonly spelled 'gin', this word referred to Aboriginal women. Although today this word is offensive, the editors have retained it in this text to reflect the historical character of the novel, as the redacting of such terms can create its own form of whitewashing. Here it reflects Fraser's two-dimensional understanding of Indigeneity.

sworn in as Justices of the Peace, so that they could mutually oblige by punishing for each other. The amount of flogging a man should have was generally decided *before* a man was sent away for the nominal trial to the neighbouring Justice of the Peace. If a squatter was busy and could not afford to have a hand laid up, the punishment was not of a disabling kind, though it might be severe. It is scarcely necessary to say – remembering the cruelty of that time – that the invariable punishment was the lash.

'Mr Beedham said that both men would probably be punished about nine o'clock the next morning and that he did not know whether or not the King's pardon would override the magistrate's award for a fault committed in the country. He, however, would be inclined to give Jacobs the benefit of the doubt, for he had been a willing servant and he had, until that afternoon, had no cause for complaint. Even in that particular case the other man was quite as likely to be to blame as Jacobs was.

'Mother was terribly anxious.

'It was night. She had twenty miles to go to be at her journey's end before her husband's appearance in court the next morning. For she wished to present the pardon and claim her husband as a free man before a local sentence of any kind was passed upon him.

'As I have previously mentioned, she could not ride. Mr Beedham had nothing lighter in the way of a conveyance than a bullock dray. All the horses were saddle horses used for boundary riding, yarding stock, etc. American buggies were not to be had in the back blocks of New South Wales in King William's day. After a good deal of talking and planning it was decided that Mother and the trooper should start about three o'clock in the morning for McCallum's, she sitting as best she could upon a horse led at walking-pace. For the distance was more than a day's journey for a bullock team, and a very rough and wearying walk for a woman who had been travelling for a week in the primitive way of the time.

'Mother would not have cared; she would have cheerfully set off at once and walked all night, but where would she have got to? There was only a track through the wilderness, no telegraph wires and no roads; she would have been hopelessly lost before she had walked two miles. In this portion of the Australian continent, there is a constant sameness in the scenery. Even in flying over it by rail or coach, the same scene keeps repeating itself: brown and almost bare plains – dry, dusty, dotted with eucalyptus. Close your eyes for an hour, look out of the carriage window again – the same scene, you have travelled twenty miles and might not have moved.

'At eight o'clock the next morning Mother and the trooper – the latter managing both horses – presented themselves at the front of a decent-sized house supposing themselves to be at the end of their journey. In this they were labouring under a mistake; they had got off the main track and had got to the house of the foreman, quite eight miles from McCallum's principal station. They found two jins in the house and one of these brought in a black who could speak a little English.

'The black was induced to go with them and act as guide lest they should again get off the track and lose more invaluable time.

'Owing to the delay it was nearly half nine when they arrived at McCallum's. Meanwhile the farce of an investigation had been made and both Father and his co-worker had been sentenced to twenty-five lashes each. They had been taken to the stockyard for punishment. Out rushed my mother, shouting, "Where is my husband?" The soreness and cramp and weariness caused by seven hours in the saddle all disappeared instantly, and Mother ran like a girl the quarter-mile distance to the yard. Yes, there was Father, faced towards her, as Mother ran calling, "Stop! Stop! A pardon! A pardon!"

'Father's face was set and his teeth clenched and he was doing his best trying to bear his utterly undeserved punishment in silence, when suddenly he heard his wife's voice, and saw running swiftly towards him the woman whom he supposed to be in England and whom he never expected to see again.

'He would have endured the lash, but the sudden revulsion of feeling produced by Mother's coming and the King's pardon proved too much and for the first time in his life he fainted.

'What had led up to this tragedy?

'Simply this: Father was what colonials term a "new chum". He did not understand and could not appreciate the ways of the community into which he had been thrown. He was too moral for his surroundings. His working companion, a convict like himself, had been on McCallum's station for several years and thoroughly understood his work. The new man was sent to work with the already trained one, and the two lived in the bark hut a dozen miles from the central house or homestead. Great numbers of the men so situated got native women, called jins, to live with them, and to prepare their rations and do what housework had to be done or could be done where the house was a bark hut twelve feet by ten or less.

'Father's mate had had a jin for several years about the hut, and she had died a few weeks before Father joined. For months after there was no jin about the place, until one day the shepherd brought in with him a young jin, apparently a girl of about twelve years of age. As Father had been cook and housemaid since his arrival he set to work to teach the new girl her duties, and took some interest in his charge. He learned a little of her language and she learned more of his, until they could understand each other pretty well. By this time the jin could do all the indoor work, and have the meals ready for the men. Father described her as a nice girl and said that she appeared more intelligent than the majority of Australian blacks.

'One evening as Father rode up to the hut he heard a series of shrill screams. He threw himself off his horse and, dashing in to see what was the matter, found the girl Nattie struggling in the arms of his mate, who was attempting something improper. Seeing Father he desisted, and the girl sheltered herself, sobbing and quivering with excitement, behind Father. Father's companion pleaded that it was the custom of the country to make the jins into slaves of that kind, and told father that he was welcome to keep one himself. Father said he had a dear wife in England, and that he would never degrade himself or his wife by any such connection, and that he would protect Nattie from outrage.

'From this time there was a deal of sullenness and ill feeling between the two men. Nattie, too, showed much aversion to Bob and took care never to be in the hut unless Father was there. So events went on until the day before Mother got to Beedham's station. Again Father had caught Bob in the act of molesting Nattie. This time he had ridden after the poor girl until she could run no longer and had caught her, panting and gasping for breath.

'Father kept his promise. Bob tried to defend himself and managed to plant a few blows on Father, but on the whole he got much the worst of the encounter. Beedham thought he understood the matter and so sent the two of them off to McCallum's station, charged with fighting for the possession of a jin and neglecting their duty. The innocent cause of all this trouble wandered about the hut for several days and saw the return of Bob, with his half-healed back, and seeing nothing of Father she went back to her tribe and her old wild life.

'When Father regained consciousness he was released from the grating, and Mother was kneeling beside him washing the blood off his torn and bruised back, upon which had fallen five of the twenty-five lashes he was sentenced to receive for protecting a girl from the mad lust of a fellow countryman.

'Fortunately Bob had been triced up the first, else Father would have received twenty more, and been rendered incapable of movement for a week at least. It was a cruel time. For mere trifles and often for no fault, men were flogged almost to death. A black pall of crime and cruelty overhung the whole land. No wonder that the settlers, a few years later, demanded their freedom from the stain of being a convict settlement. No writer will dare to depict the social life of the time. Marcus Clarke[3]

---

3 English-born journalist Clarke (1846–1881) emigrated to Victoria in 1863. His magnum opus, *For the Term of His Natural Life* (1870-1872), is esteemed as a masterful psychological insight into the colony's punitive world, although its historical value has been extensively critiqued. See: Graeme Davison, 'Clarke, Marcus Andrew Hislop,' in Graeme Davison, John Hirst and Stuart Macintyre (eds.), *The Oxford Companion to Australian History* (Melbourne: Oxford University Press, 1998), 129–130.

has given some phases of it as applied to Tasmania, and his pages are harrowing in the extreme.[4]

'Father soon got better. Freedom and the presence of his dearly loved wife made him forget his pains. In ten days from that memorable morning, we all met in Sydney again. We were as poor us ever, or nearly so, but we were all healthy, happy and free from the stigma of crime. Mother's journey was over.'

4 Footnote in original: Says one man who had business in Bathurst Courthouse, 'I saw a man walk across the yard with the blood that had run from his lacerated flesh squashing out of his shoes at every step he took. A dog was licking the blood off the triangles and the ants were carrying away great pieces of human flesh that the lash had scattered about the ground. The scourger's foot had worn a deep hole in the ground by the violence with which he whirled himself round on it to strike the quivering and wealed back, out of which stuck the sinews, white, ragged and swollen. The infliction was one hundred lashes at half-minute time, so as to extend the punishment through nearly an hour. The day was hot enough to overcome a man merely standing that length of time in the sun, and this was going on in the full blaze of it. However, they had a pair of scourgers who gave each other spell and spell about, and they were bespattered with blood like a couple of butchers.'

CHAPTER III

YOUTH AND EARLY MANHOOD

OUR HERO'S DIARY is pretty full of particulars as to the settling of his family and their progress in the new country, but his story for the next few years is not very sensational or out of the common run of experience. The Government authorities gave the pardoned man a choice between a passage home and a small grant of land in the vicinity of the infant city. His parents chose the latter, and the father and mother, for many years, made a good living by keeping a few cows and growing vegetables.

The elder girls got married early, the other two children came from England. On the whole, things went well with the family of Jacobs. If they had held on to the piece of land granted by the Government, their descendants today would have been very rich. As it was, they were much better off than they could ever have hoped to be in England. The old man lived to be seventy, and his wife nursed her great-grandchildren and was alive in Sydney in 1875. We have nothing more to do with the family life. None of them either made a fortune or attained distinction. They lived simple and honest lives, such as their ancestors in Lancashire had done for generations.

Adam Jacobs worked for a time with his parents and made himself useful as a farmer and gardener until he was about eighteen years of age. He then joined a shipping firm and underwent some adventures while sailing in the South Sea Islands and trading with the Māori in the North Island of New Zealand. Some of his scrapes and escapes would bear recording, and would be given a place in his book if they had not been eclipsed by late adventures of much greater importance that must be recorded.

When about twenty-three years of age we find him running a small business of his own as ship chandler and outfitter, and his diary gives a few hints regarding a powerful incentive to settle down and remain ashore in the form of a blue-eyed daughter of a sea captain whom he frequently visits. Business is successfully prosecuted. He builds a small suburban villa – suburb and villa long since swallowed up in city and forgotten – and at twenty-four becomes a benedict[5], marrying a woman who for more than forty years proves a true helpmeet and faithful companion. We have not done with her. We meet her again many times and do not part with her until the diary, and the story, comes to an end.

Business fluctuates and Jacobs grows impatient. He hears of the rapid growth of Melbourne. He goes to Melbourne to establish a branch of his business and the branch rapidly becomes the leading house, so much so that he moves to

---

5 A 'benedict' is a recently married man; from the character of the same name in Shakespeare's *Much Ado about Nothing*.

the new city in the earlier part of 1842. Before the end of the year, however, there is a grand collapse in commercial and financial circles. A land boom, which has been leading to some artificial successes and giving a fictitious value to everything, suddenly bursts up and a kind of universal bankruptcy sets in.

Jacobs is involved like many others and declares himself bankrupt on the same day that Melbourne declares itself to be a city and claims municipal rights.

For nine years more the diaries record little but the struggles of a businessman trying to earn an honest living without much capital to back him up. He has to give credit and to take produce instead of cash, the coin of the realm being a scarce article everywhere. However, he and his wife work together in their store and make their position tolerable again.

And now comes the gold find in Bathurst, and Jacobs, hearing of the rapid acquisition of wealth by lucky diggers, must try his luck. His wife keeps the business going in the almost empty city, and Jacobs searches for gold and finds a rheumatic fever, of which he nearly dies, and comes home a sad wreck to be nursed into health again.

He has barely recovered when gold is found near Melbourne, and the rushes to Ballarat and Mount Alexander take place. Ten thousand miners are washing out gold within sixty miles of Melbourne. This time our diarist follows the rush to supply provisions to the diggers and finds that pays better than digging.

Some of his records about this time are full of adventure. He gets his drays bogged and the bullocks sink into the ground until only their heads are visible. He tells of the roads becoming so bad that a pound of flour has to be sold for two shillings in order that the cost of its carriage may be defrayed. He does not speak of the miners as a lawless set of men at all. They seem to be anxious to wash out plenty of dust, and indeed they have to in order to live when they are fed but poorly at a cost of about a sovereign a day.

Of course there was a contingent of roughs, but these were kept in check by the stern, rough-and-ready justice dealt out by the more orderly members of the community. There was a mixture of all classes – sailors, soldiers, university scholars, tradesmen, businessmen and even British peers. The Marquis of Salisbury spent some time in the Victorian goldfields.

Jacobs going to and fro with money and goods was never robbed and never subjected to personal violence. On the contrary, he frequently speaks of the help he gets from most unlikely quarters when he gets into difficulties. On one occasion four diggers worked 'up to the eyes in mud' for nearly a day extricating him and his stores, his four bullocks and his dray from a morass, and all he can prevail upon them to accept is each a bottle of beer and a cake of tobacco. Judging from Jacobs's diary, the accounts of the lawlessness of the goldfields have been much exaggerated.

In this diary a mere passing mention is made of the separation of Victoria from New South Wales. The great influx of population which occurred at this time, and a few years afterwards, does not appear to have had much effect upon the fortunes of Jacobs. He seems to have stuck to the goldfields trade too long, to have gone on with it after the rush was over, and to have made losses in the latter part of the time. For we find in the diary for 1858, on his fortieth birthday, he remarks, 'I am now forty years of age. It is said that what a man is at forty he will be all his life. If so, I shall be a poor struggling man to the end of my term, for I have never been worth a thousand pounds in my life, although I have had as good chances as many of the men who have made fortunes. Too soon or too late I have ever been. If I had given up this travelling business two years ago and let the debts slide, I would have been hundreds of pounds in pocket.'

He gives up the goldfields, leaves to more active and enterprising men the work of following up the new rushes and comes back to town. His children are getting useful in the store and his wife proves herself the better businessman of the two. As a result, he is at liberty to devote attention to any other pursuit by which he can earn a bit of money. So he commences as a commission agent and now thirty years later he is still so engaged.

No breach ever happened between Jacobs and his wife, although she took the lead in the city business, and ran it for over twenty years with the help of the children. The very saddest pages in his diaries are those in which he records the death of his wife, which occurred in his sixty-fifth year.

The business which he founded, and which his wife put her life into, is carried on in the city to this day by one of his children.

Taken as a whole the life appears to be a commonplace one; just a straight and simple life such as might be lived by anyone. Had this been all, however, the story of Jacobs would never have been lifted out of the dusty obscurity of his accumulated diaries.

CHAPTER IV

Strange Dreams

Writing in the year 1863, his forty-fifth year, Jacobs tells of a few months of illness and of a low nervous condition into which he drops as a result of that illness. He never entirely recovers. He is often absent-minded and he needs much more sleep than he used to require. His hard life has evidently told upon him and the grand climacteric has come early.

He writes: 'I had a strange dream last night, a series of strange sensations mostly painful and terribly real. I was struggling in the dark towards some end and great forces were pitching behind and around me, and I, ever trying to escape, worked in the same direction, until at last I emerged into a blaze of light and a cold air that made me pant and gasp for a long time until I got relief, and cried out loudly for help. No sooner had I called than strong and gentle hands grasped me, and using soothing appliances made me comfortable, and then in my dream I went to sleep.'

This experience is never repeated, but for several months he dreams that he is a little child, and all the time, his surroundings are the same. He is frequently listening to sounds that he only understands in part and to music which he tries to imitate. No sooner is he asleep then he is on the knees of a gentle giantess, whom he learns to call Mother. Sometimes he appears to pass hours lying on soft, white substances, and playing with any little object that he can grasp. A few months after the first of his strange dreams we find the record of his idea.

'I am at length forced to the conclusion that I have been somewhere else, and am living the life of a happy, healthy baby in a most comfortable and cheerful home. Everything is built to that scale. The people about me are giants in relation to me because of my own littleness. I know several people, and am talked to and played with by first one then another. I am never tossed about, no one ever frightens me. I am learning to talk and begin to understand much of what is said to me. I can get about in a tumbling sort of way and might walk if I did not get tripped up by so many things. There is a bright warm fire, but I can never reach it. I am even puzzled to know where I am. There are certainly many things about me that would not be about me if I were a baby in Melbourne, or in any country that I know. Were I to tell anyone that I am at once a man of middle age and a baby in the arms, I should be regarded as qualified for a lunatic asylum. Am I in what is called dotage? Do old people who become childish do so because they are children elsewhere?'

The diaries now contain scarcely anything but a record of what he no longer regards as a dream. He says little of business and not much of domestic life. He only works a few hours daily and is frequently absent-minded. He attends spiritualistic meetings and reads the literature of people who try to pierce the clouds surrounding birth, life and death. He analyses his memories and feelings, and comes to the conclusion that he is living a dual life, but is only half conscious of its duality, inasmuch as he can remember here what occurs in the new life, but cannot in the new life remember anything that happens in the old one.

He philosophises thus: 'Are all children rejuvenations and is the old life always forgotten in the new one? Is the soul always rising on a new life when setting on an old one? If so, what becomes of the souls of infants and those of people killed by accident early in life? Is the memory of the previous life or lives always obliterated by death and birth or by birth and death, whichever happens first? Do our odd sensations and impressions regarding people and places arise from an imperfect memory of something that we passed through in a previous life? We meet a stranger and at once like or dislike in an unreasoning manner – is that stranger one who has strongly influenced us for good or evil in some previous existence? We come to a place that we have never visited and find it quite familiar; we expect at the next turn of the road, a tree, house, or lake, and, lo, it is there – is this a memory that has survived?'

He reads stories of ubiquity and wonders if it is common for people to be in two places at one time. About this, too, he makes remarks, but these are not quoted here, as he speaks with fuller knowledge later on. He has already got to thinking that there is more in birth, life and death than appears on the surface. He thinks that fissipation[6] may be a possibility.

'There are lives capable of division. Split the living organism into two and they each begin an individual life.

6 This term was used in biology to refer to reproduction by fission.

Instead of killing by division, we have made one creature into two. Is this in some way possible in higher structures? Have I undergone the process known to naturalists as fissipation?'

Meanwhile the days go on and the dream that has taken such a hold upon the life of our hero is unfolding itself rapidly. If he is living two lives, there is a great difference between them. One is almost devoid of events of note and changes; the other passes into new experiences and fresh knowledge daily. He runs about now and talks and plays with other children and finds something new to see and think about every day. He is a very happy child in dreamland and there he is not conscious of his duality – not yet.

One morning he wakes up with the knowledge that he is two years old. There has been a gathering of several of his playfellows, there has been music and games during a pleasant summer afternoon, his mother and father looking on and joining in the fun. Several friends, too, have called and all have reminded him that he is two years old. He turns back the pages of his diary and finds that his dream-life has lasted nearly four years – how is it then that he is only two years old in the new life?

Has he been born into some part of the world where time is reckoned differently? That cannot be – a year is a year wherever time is reckoned, there may be differences in the naming of months, may be differences in the time of commencing the year, numbering of the years, and other minor particulars, but the duration of the year is the same; a child has not to live nearly four years in order to be two years old. In China a child is called one year old when born, but he is conscious that he is not in China, and conscious, too, that he is amongst people who are exceptionally happy and prosperous; who are very beautiful to look upon; who are never sick or weary, never poor nor ill-clad; and whose surroundings are harmonious and pleasant in a high degree. The people themselves also never quarrel nor say bitter things of each other when absent. Where on the Earth can this state of things be found? What child can live through infancy without seeing something of sickness, pain, poverty, without knowing something of vice or evil speaking?

'Where am I?' says our hero. 'Are my sleeping hours spent in Heaven? That cannot be, for Heaven is an abode of spirits and my dream-land is an abode of tangible bodies. I have as active, healthy a little body as anyone could wish; and my father and mother, my playfellows and friends, and all the things around us, are real enough and familiar to me. And yet life is different and the people are different, and there are many things about that would not be found in the best houses in Melbourne or in London. Our fires are warm and bright and keep the rooms pleasant, and yet they never burn anything. In royal households, so far as I know, there are no such fires. At night we have no lamps and yet light comes from luminous points in walls and ceilings, and I can only once remember being in the dark and then I had done a rare thing – had wakened in the night.

'Am I on Earth? If so, not in any part I have heard or read of. I am not in the Christian's Heaven, for I am not dead; on the contrary I appear to be too much alive, to be living two lives while the majority of the people have to be content with one. There must have been a millennium where I have strayed to, for all the imaginings of the poets and dreamers are more than realised, there is no sin nor sorrow where I live – but I am only two years old and it has taken me nearly four years to reach that age – where am I?'

This is the first time that Jacobs asks his whereabouts; the dates have set him off. The answer to his question becomes easy enough in a while and we will not run into future pages of his diary in order to answer his question now.

A few days after this strange second birthday, we find a report of a talk with his mother. The mother appears to be the leading spirit in the daily life of the family, of his dream-father we hear little. He describes himself as standing by his mother's knee in an oval-shaped room, an upper room of a strangely shaped house. Not strange in shape to the child, but to the man. Her hand is toying with his curls and she is saying, 'My dear boy is now two years old and has therefore reached the age of moral responsibility. He is no longer an infant, but a child who understands many things and knows when he is doing right. He can always appeal to Mother for counsel and help, but he is now accounted as responsible to his own conscience and to the Giver of all Good for his actions. So far my boy's life has been all happiness and pleasure; he has not known that wrong is possible, nor that there are such things as temptation and sin. His life will probably be spent amongst good people who are devoid of pride and envy, but temptation of some kind is sure to arise and my boy will have to do right under all circumstances. As he is two years of age my boy must begin his educational course also. This will begin tomorrow.'

'Did you go to school when you were two, Mother?'

'Yes, I did.'

'And how old are you now, Mother?'

'I am nearly fourteen. There, now, my boy can go and play with Emma for a little while, and he will join Hildreth's class tomorrow.'

This is the first mention of his sister Emma, who is at this period half his age. He mentions no older child, so he must have been the first born in dream-land.

CHAPTER V

School Days

'WHEN MOTHER TOLD me that I had to join Hildreth's class, she did not threaten me. Hildreth is a teacher of infants and she makes all infants who come to her desire to do so. I had had many a game of romps with her and she had entirely won my young heart. About twenty of us next morning met in Hildreth's classroom. Not more than twenty-five pupils were allowed to any teacher, and I found out that there were many teachers who, like Hildreth, had the affection of every child present.

'Our lessons were mostly a series of easy movements – marching and singing. We threw hoops with pairs of sticks and caught other hoops with the same sticks. We played with balls and we taught each other to build houses. Hildreth played music for us and showed us how to move in musical time.

'Each child had a recess with shelves, upon which it kept its tools and toys. I had to learn now to get mine and put them all in their places when done with. We were kept under control all morning and yet were only sorry that the school time was over. There are a great number of pretty things in my recess, the uses of which I do not yet know.'

In this part of the diary there are many pages of rather vague description, such as that just quoted. But from it we gather that the teacher has the art of interesting children and enlisting their affections, and that the system of instruction is eminently suitable for children, for their faculties are always pleasantly on the alert and their minds and bodies are constantly occupied. Whatever the teacher does, each child has to do and furthermore it has to understand why. One child is never pushed forward at the expense of the others, and if one child in the class is a little dull, both teacher and sharper pupils pay especial attention and keep it in pace with the rest.

No child was ever asked to remember anything or to repeat anything, and yet each child knew in a little while how to make each sign it had to copy and what it meant, and the knowledge remained and grew and never became a burden.

In two years, all but about six weeks from the time of joining Hildreth's class, he reports himself as three years old, and as having finished his infant school course. He does not on this occasion express any wonder at the apparent confusion of dates. He is, however, engaged in astronomical studies, and comes to the truth in due time.

He reports progress thus: 'It does not fall to the lot of many men to have been twice educated as a child, and to be able to remember both methods and compare results. As a child I appear to know more now at three years of age, or reckoning by our time about five years and nine months, than I knew at ten years of age, the time I left school in my first childhood. I can read and write with perfect ease, and yet I never had to learn an alphabet or the spelling of any word. I can do many kinds of calculating mentally, and yet never committed to memory any table. It is the same with weights, measures and periods of time, a knowledge of them seems to have grown into my mind. I have not forgotten anything I have learned, and what I have learned is so intertwined with what I have done that one invariably suggests the other.

'In calculating we had each an abacus with one hundred beads upon it, and could add, subtract, multiply and divide small sums, and then we were shown the relationship between these calculations and those on our little boards.

'It amused us very much to add up several sums on the abacus by placing the beads and then to do the same work in figures. We had no rules to learn; we simply extended the work done on the abacus by slow degrees. And as all things in my dream-land are calculated by tens and tenths, the ten tens on the abacus can evidently be made to help in all kinds of calculations.

'It was just as easy to learn to read and write, for we had only to learn a new sign when we wanted to represent a new sound, and vice versa, each sign having its sound and each sound its sign, none being interchangeable or liable to modification by preceding or succeeding ones. It seemed as if in everything the knowledge was allowed to grow in us and compelled to become part of us. We had to work out all that we learned. When we had learned how to measure a square we had to measure it on the boards or in the school field. As a child in dream-life this appears natural. It is only when I compare my dream education with the one I should get if I were again an infant in waking life that I perceive the immense advantage of my dream-life mode of receiving instruction.'

Evidently our diarist has got into some Utopia. Reformers have tried to alter our written language and to make education easier for children, but in no part of the world have these results been so fully accomplished as in this land. The children are not quite angels even here, for in Hildreth's class punishment has to be inflicted. He writes: 'One day, when I had learned to make several kinds of buildings out of my box of various-shaped blocks, I took a fancy to erect a larger building, and for this purpose I took several of my neighbour's blocks when his attention was turned away. Hildreth was not long in seeing my trick and coming to the rescue. I knew I had done wrong and felt very guilty, but cannot recollect being afraid. So far I had never wittingly done wrong and had never seen anyone suffer punishment. I began to put back the blocks I had borrowed. When I took them I had no intention of keeping them, so that my crime was borrowing without leave, not actual theft.

'Hildreth did not ask me if I had taken any blocks; she simply told me to put those I had taken into a certain separate heap. This done, she called the whole class and pointed out what I had done. I felt very much ashamed and began to cry, so did Frank, my victim, and several others.

'The class-mother – for that was what we called her – then asked us to tell her the kind of fault I was guilty of. My peers were not accustomed to crimes and could come to no definite conclusion. Hildreth helped them to come to the conclusion that I had been guilty of selfishness and that I had acted in a greedy manner by taking the blocks without asking for them. She did not call my action a crime; that in itself would have been too great a punishment. I was already more an object of pity than of anger.

'My fault had to be punished, and the class had to devise my punishment. Not one suggested the infliction of any kind of physical pain. Indeed, I had never heard of pain at this time as inflicted by one person upon another. One said, "Take his blocks from him." Another, a sharp-eyed little girl, the least in the class, said, "No, let us give him plenty of blocks, he can have all mine." "And mine," "and mine," ran round the class. Hildreth consented and in another minute I had more than twenty boxes of blocks. The class work went on another hour and I felt very miserable. My sudden accession of wealth was a most painful experience. I did not want to play with blocks, my architectural ambitions were entirely scattered. For the first time my recess would not hold my possessions. I was the richest boy in the class and each day I had to carry out the blocks and build, those who had no blocks looking on. I never opened any of the added boxes and only built up a few forms listlessly out of my own and was glad to carry them all back again.

'At the end of four days, I was allowed to return to each of my classmates his own box and to put mine in its proper place. I learned then once and for all never to covet useless wealth, and to rest content with my own share. The punishment was in the line of my fault and made me heartily ashamed of selfishness and greed.

'I told my mother all about the proceedings of each day. She did not make much comment. Evidently she knew I was in good hands. When it was all over she took me into her oval chamber and explained my fault. What she told me seemed quite correct then and there, but hardly harmonises with my waking experience.

"The blocks and the other articles you use in the class are not yours; they are only there for your use as long as you need them. In a little while you will go to another class and find other toys, tools and books, and will leave these you now have to your successor. It is so with everything; nobody has any private property in anything except personal belongings, such as clothes. If your father was wanted at some other place and was willing to go – he would not have to go otherwise – we should leave this home, and all in it, and have another equally good to go to. But nothing here is absolutely ours; we could take nothing with us except what I tell you."

"Could we take Father's new picture?" said I, looking at a new artistic production that seemed to be a living and conscious presentation of Father.

"Yes, that is our own."

"And your new travelling robe, is that yours?"

"As long as I want it, yes, it is mine. But if I had no further need for it, and it was still good and nice, I would take it to the depot, so that another woman if she required it could wear it. We do this so that unused articles may not rot and go to waste."

"Our flying fish?"

"That, too, is ours while we use it. It cost a great amount of labour to produce it and is on that account very valuable. If your father were not a highly skilled workman, he would not have so valuable an article for his sole use, in that case we should travel by the public air fish. There, now, ask no more questions. I will tell you more by-and-by; you are only a little boy yet. You will remember not to be selfish any more. Give me a kiss and go help Emma with her pretty picture puzzles.'"

Our diarist has evidently got into a land where a number of ideas have got worked into practical shape. Real estate is only held by those who use it. There is no property except in personal belongings and even these must not be heaped up and kept to rot. Several things tend to arouse his curiosity, but he is bound to wait. If he could make himself equally conscious in both spheres he might ask for information, but hitherto he can remember nothing of his old life in his new one, although he can remember all that happens in the new life while in the waking one. Indeed, the dream-land memories haunt his waking hours and make him absent-minded and odd in manner.

One evening he writes: 'I have been all day bothering my head about the flying fishes I mentioned the other day. They are always going about in the air. I can never look up without seeing some. They are so common that no one appears to notice them. It is not long since we got one of our own. Sister Emma and I were in the garden, where we grow a great number of highly coloured flowers, when we heard a familiar voice overhead. We looked up and there was Father on a flying fish descending in a spiral curve almost upon us. The fish came lightly to the ground with all its fins folded, and Father got out. He and Mother carried it into a long, narrow house, built on purpose for it.

'Next day we all went flying. Inside the fish was almost like a boat. Father sat at one end, Mother at the other, Emma and I were in between. We were told to keep still, and then Father pulled out some little knobs and the fish began to rise spirally, as if climbing on an immense screw, until it got a certain height, and then its fins came out to the full length and made great sweeping strokes, and we went forward fast, very fast. I could not breathe when looking in the direction we were going. We could see through the floor, and looking down everything seemed to be in rapid motion, running away behind us. There were other fishes, too, that kept crossing above and below us in all directions.

'When we had been flying some time we dropped in the same spiral way and spent the afternoon with some friends. When we came back it was night and our fish had its eyes made into a pair of great lamps. I have no idea of how we got home or when. Emma and I were wrapped in a soft, warm rug and must have gone to sleep. What is this fish? It has feathery-looking fans about the tail, and these move up and down and from right to left as we steer, and we have two pairs of wing-like fins at the sides. There is no smoke and no noise. In my dream-life – I still call it "dream-life" though it is as real as any life can be – I have no consciousness of my waking life or I would ask some questions. It is possible that if I had such consciousness it might interfere with my happiness and growth as a child. The idea of a child of five being conscious of living else-where as a man of fifty.

'At the same time there may be some sort of filtering of one life into the other for one day. I asked Mother if Father earned much money.

"Money, child! What do you mean?"

"Money that people work for, and that they pay for things with," I answered.

"Well, my boy, that is about the strangest question you have ever asked. Where have you seen any money? Who has spoken to you of money?"

"I don't know, Mother; somehow the question came."

'That afternoon I heard Mother and Father talking about the question, and Father said that money transactions had ceased more than ten thousand years before, and that I could not have either heard or read of money. Mother sat awhile thinking, and then remarked, "Perhaps he is an Earthborn, and that was an idea from the inferior world."'

About a week later our diarist writes: 'I have to go to school again. Not to Hildreth's – I have finished with her class, to my sorrow – but to Harry Gaston's, which is held in the same block of buildings. I know Gaston and like him, and as several of my previous classmates go with me to Gaston's, I may be as happy there as I was with Hildreth. What a strange record! Have I to dream myself through another school course? Shall I learn where my lot is cast? Shall I become equally conscious in both lives?'

CHAPTER VI

GASTON'S CLASS

'FOR SEVERAL DAYS now I have been a pupil of Gaston's. He is a bright-eyed, cheerful man, and is always in a smiling and happy mood. He leads us all to ask questions, and makes our lessons a treat. As before, each pupil has a recess, in which is found all that is required both for the school and the playfields. The box of blocks is gone and in its place there are a lot of pieces of wood of various forms. The abacus is replaced by one, the beads of which have double wires that hold them so that figures and cyphers stamped upon them are always in sight. It has another peculiarity. A wire runs perpendicularly across the centre, keeping the beads half to the right and half to the left. An elder boy, one who has been in Gaston's class for some time, caught me pondering over the new abacus. He explained it to me, saying that the perpendicular wire was the decimal point, and that the beads to the left went up by powers of ten, and those to the right went down by tenths, hundredths, etc. That small white square let into the bead is meant to hold a figure. However you will soon find all that out.'

It will not be wise to burden these pages with all the incidents and accidents that happen to a sharp boy in a primary school, even under the tuition of a teacher like Gaston, aided as he is by models and illustrations and samples of natural productions and manufactured goods. The class is willing to learn, is eager to listen and to look, and gather up the knowledge that the teacher is so able to impart. In school hours there is no listlessness, no weariness, no heavy task, nor are there any lessons to carry home. There is no spelling to learn, no tables to commit to memory, and all school work is done in school hours.

They go to school once a day, and spend four hours in school work. After an hour and a half of study the class goes through several of the exercises learned in Hildreth's class, and some new ones, all set to music, and many of them accompanied with song. In this way half-an-hour is spent and they study another hour and a half. That done, they go into the playfield with the whole school and play as they like with entire freedom for half-an-hour. The last hour is spent in reading, writing from dictation, and if any child is puzzled or in doubt about a lesson, Gaston will answer questions at his desk during this hour.

Five hours at school and nothing to eat! Poor children. Our diarist says little about food so far, but a little later on he says the people in general have only one meal daily, but that children have a little food early in the day and their next meal with their elders early in the afternoon when all work ceases.

One accident happens which is worth recording, since it might easily have proved fatal and stopped the records of this very real dream-land:

'I had been in Gaston's class for about three months (Earth-time) when one afternoon early we all went for a journey in our flying fish. We had all got used to it now and I frequently looked over the sides at the houses and beautiful gardens below us. The land beneath us was a perfect paradise of beauty. The houses nestled amongst their trees, nearly all of which were fruit-bearing and the interspersed flower gardens glowed radiant with all the colours of the sunrise, the sunset and the rainbow. There was nothing trim and chessboard-like in the appearance of the ground, and at the same time there were no roads and no disorderly open spaces. Every inch of the land was utilised. Oh the delight of floating through that perfumed summer air free from dust, smoke, noise and all the disagreeables we would have if floating at about three hundred feet above an Earth town, or even village. No jarring, grating sounds, only the sound of musical voices now and then, with snatches of song.

'We were approaching a clear lake, smooth as a mirror, reflecting some trees that grew on its further side so clearly that every leaf and twig that grew upward in the air appeared to grow downward in the water. We crossed the lake, flying slowly and enjoying the scene. When about halfway over I looked down over the side, and saw the reflection of our air boat with its fins or wings sweeping to and fro slowly and silently. I had no idea before how graceful the machine looked when in motion. I leaned over a little and called Mother to see how pretty the reflection. She moved towards me, not to look, but to seize my clothing. The slight oscillation caused by her movement brought about what she feared, for over I went. For a little while I remember feeling the air rush past me and seeing the tops of the trees coming to meet me. And then something touched my back; an instant more and I was firmly clenched by my clothing. My father had followed me down in the machine and caught me. But he was too late to get up into the air again. Our wings were tangled in the tree top and one of them in its final stroke knocked me out of Father's hand. "Clutch the branches," said he, as I dropped into the foliage. I tried to do so and broke my fall materially. I do not remember getting to the ground.

~

'I next remember waking out of a pleasant sleep and finding myself in Mother's oval chamber. Two voices were speaking gently, one was my mother's and the other was strange to me. I was the subject of their remarks. Perhaps I ought to have uttered some sound, but I just lay there dreamily trying to find out how I had got there and listening to bits of the conversation now and then.

"You think, then, that what my little boy has said in his wanderings really proves him an Earthborn?"

"Yes, and more than that. They prove him to be living a dual life. On Earth he must be a man of middle age, for he speaks to his children as if upgrown and his peers."

"How strange to have a child like that. He is old enough to be his mother's father. Is my experience unique, or are there many such?"

"My studies in medical psychology have taught me that there are three kinds of Earthborns on our planet. First, those who have lived on Earth and become fit for introduction to our higher life, which is to them a kind of heaven and reward for virtuous and religious living;

49

second, those who, while still living on Earth, put out a new life and live here also quite unconscious of the old life; third, those who live on both planets, and are conscious of the two lives. Your boy belongs to the second class at present, but can at any time begin to belong to the third. In his Earth life he is conscious of this life, but in this he is unconscious of the other."

"Perhaps not quite so. He was asking me about money not long ago. He cannot have heard of money here. From whence came the money question?"

"It came like many other questions asked by children out of the past and out of the deep. Before we know whence such questions spring we shall have to know from where the life of the questioner springs."

"To return to this question of dual identity. How does the soul animate two bodies and get from one to the other? My boy is never absent-minded. I have had no reason to suspect him of being anywhere else but here."

"There are thousands of mysteries of the soul of which we know nothing, but if we were to question your son some day we might get an answer to your question. In similar cases people have been sent into a magnetic trance and have said that for the soul there are no such limitations as time and space, that it can be where it will when it will, that the author of the soul's being can alone regulate or limit its movements."

"Then my son can fly from one body to the other, the two bodies being on different planets at enormous and ever-varying distances apart, without much loss of time?"

"Without any loss. It would take you a thousand times as long to walk through that open door into this room as it will take him to come from the other side of the solar system."

"Thank you, doctor. I fear I have taken up too much of your valuable time with my questionings. After all, I am so much the mother that I am glad to hear that, but for a little stiffness and pain, my boy will be well when he wakes."

'At this moment I made some movement and hurt my side, and cried out with the pain. I had never felt pain before. My cry brought Mother and her companion to my side. Mother bade me be still and keep quiet, and Doctor Hildreth, the physician for our district, Class-mother Hildreth's sister, looked into my eyes, and felt my pulse, and said to Mother, "He is quite out of danger; he needs no further aid from me."

'When the doctor had gone, Mother told me that in falling through the tree I had broken two ribs and got much bruised, and had been unconscious for several days, owing to having fallen upon my head. She told me that if I did not wish my wounds to hurt me, I must keep still and they would soon heal.

'In the next few days I found that Father's hands had been cut with the last stroke of the wing of our air boat while trying to hold me up, and that if he had not let me fall into the tree I should probably have been killed by the same blow. Mother had clutched Emma and held on until rescued by another air boat, and our flying fish had suffered serious damage and gone to be repaired.'

From this it appears that accidents may happen even in the grand world of our diarist's dreams. A day or two later he resumes his narrative: 'I am back in Gaston's class. All my classmates have congratulated me on my fortunate escape. I begin to feel that I am of some importance in the world. Gaston notices the state of things and wisely puts me right, and makes my case a lesson at the same time. This, too, without hurting my feelings.

'He says: "You are very properly glad to see Charlie Frankston amongst you after his narrow escape from death, and he doubtless rejoiced to find himself with you again. Do not, however, make too much of a hero of Charlie. There was nothing heroic about the transaction except the bravery and skill exhibited by his father in saving his life, which he undoubtedly did, although he could not prevent the final little fall through the tree. Charlie's part was just that of a careless and curious little boy, and what he did perilled the life of all his family. Let us hope that the lesson he has received may last him for life.

"Had Charlie's father been going in any other direction, he would have caught Charlie before he got to the tree tops. For the air boat can be made to descend faster than a falling body. If there had been more room and time, the boat would have gone under Charlie, and still descending, would have caught him without stopping his fall too rapidly. Some of you know the air boat rules of flight. To the north three hundred feet, to the south six hundred feet, to the east nine hundred feet, and to the west twelve hundred feet.

"When the accident happened Charlie's family were going north, and so could not fly at a height of more than three hundred feet. The manometer in the air boat, or flying fish, as it is frequently called, always indicates the height, and the compass the direction. Before these rules were made and strictly enforced accidents were frequent. They are now rare. A swift moving boat may give a slower one a push in the back, but the overtaking boat has to pass to the right, and is held as in fault if it damages the slower one. Special boats may travel in any direction and at any rate in the upper air. Below twelve hundred feet the boats travel at right angles and changing direction change height. They are also limited as to speed, not being allowed to go more than a mile a minute[7]."'

For some months now, nearly a year, our diarist's days are much alike. To record them as they are mentioned would be tiresome to writer and reader. They are the days of a schoolboy who is fond of his studies, his teacher and his classmates, and whose whole life is harmonious, happy and healthy.

The air boat is repaired and the family takes afternoon trips as before, Charlie being more careful now. The summer is passed and preparations are being made for the coming winter. Incidentally we find that the school week is only four days and that the fifth is a rest day from all work and is regarded as a Sabbath. The temporary consciousness of Earth-life in the new life that he manifested when injured has not been repeated, so that he can only set down the experiences that come in the ordinary way and can be remembered.

But now comes winter, an important event for the quickening faculties of a boy of nearly four years, each year counting almost double our three hundred and sixty-five days.

Winter is twice as long as an Earth winter, and more than twice as severe on a planet that receives only four-ninths as

---

7 Footnote in original: The mile mentioned by Gaston is probably the mile of the new world which, our diarist later on tells us, is one ten-thousandth the diameter of the planet – short of four thousand of our miles. The new mile, therefore, is about one third of ours, and the distance per hour allowed somewhere near thirty-three Earth miles – a very respectable speed.

much heat and light as our own. No wonder that Charlie's mother and father are busy storing up food in the larder and getting out and airing the soft, warm winter clothing and outdoor wraps. It is a busy time, but no one seems unhappy or anxious. All work cheerfully, as preparing for a season that brings its own pleasures.

Speaking of this approaching winter Jacobs says: 'I can remember last winter quite well. The weather was very cold, and I was not allowed to be out of doors much. During part of it I was attending Hildreth's class. I remember that I used to slide on rough ice that had grass underneath it and that we tumbled about and made merry. Our house was always warm and so was the classroom, but the out-door life was very cold. If we were not running about and sliding, we had to hurry indoors.

'This winter I am going to have skates, and Father has taken the flying fish back to the depot and got a sleigh in its place. I asked Father who was going to draw the sleigh and he pointed out a machine underneath, which he said would do that very easily and for any distance. In my waking hours I cannot understand these machines. They seem natural enough to my dream-life. There must be some great force in the air boat to move it at the speed at which it travels, carrying all of us and now the sleigh. It is not steam. It moves in silence and never shows a trace of smoke or heat. I have never seen a coal or a piece of firewood; nothing is burnt. Mother touches a knob and we have a warm fire glowing in the stove, another and the room is beautifully lit, although there is no flame and no brilliant point of light visible. Many things appear more perfect in my dream-world than in my waking one.

'Hard frost has set in, snow has fallen. Early this morning my father told me we would try my new skates this afternoon if the weather did not get too cold. I hurried home from school and we all had dinner, after which we got into the sleigh and all slid along over the white snow. We were not long in reaching the very lake into which I had almost dropped last summer. How different the scene and yet how exhilarating. All is life and graceful motion. Thousands of skaters, of both sexes and all ages, are gliding rapidly and easily about, while a band discourses sweet and lively music on the shore. They all look happy, and all seem to enter into their enjoyments heartily, as if they were entirely free from suffering and care. The elder people, and there are many here, are just as bright and happy looking as the younger ones. Even those who sit in their sleighs and watch, and those who prefer walking to gliding, have all the same happy look, a look that tells of content and happiness, of something more than the mere pleasure of the day.

'As for the music, that attends everything. We are a very musical people, so much so that our lives may be said to be set to music. It is as if we were constantly expressing our joy in thankful song.

'My father has got his skates and mine firmly fixed and away we go on the ice, he holding me up when my feet fly apart or run before me or behind me, leaving me to tumble but for his firm hand. At last we come to a comparatively quiet corner and Father, taking a seat on the bank, bids me strike out for myself. This I do, again and again coming to grief most times, but falling lightly and not hurting myself much. After another run behind Father, who gives me the end of a scarf to hold on by, we go to Mother and the sleigh and away home.

'Our home life seems easy and happy as compared with that of my earlier childhood. Lights and fires give no work. Mother has only one meal to cook. There are no dusty streets; smoke, dirt and dust are almost unknown things. Labour-saving appliances of all kinds are freely used in household work, so that taken altogether the wife and mother has no need to work much longer than the husband and father. The winter evenings we spent very pleasantly. Sometimes we had visitors, at others we visited our friends. We had merry games – games of chance and skill, reading, impersonations, dramatic and musical performances, dancing, calisthenics. All the people had plenty of time and opportunity for self-improvement, and most of them took care to excel in some accomplishment. First-class teachers of all the arts gave lessons to those who wished without any charge upon their labour. That is, all tuition of every kind is absolutely free.

'All other things are free to all appearance in some sense. At the depots we get all we want for asking. Only there is this difference: an account is kept with each responsible person or each head of a family and his production balanced with his consumption. All consumed by an individual or family is practically paid for by the labour or production of the individual or family, and generally the account is much in favour of the worker, for there are no profits. The State is the only middleman, and the costs of carriage and storage and distribution are the only additions made to prime cost. The difference between lessons and personal necessaries is this – the former are not entered against his account, the latter are.

'Teachers, lecturers, doctors, writers, actors, musicians, preachers – in short, all who work for the amusement, instruction and healing of humanity – are provided for by the State, and when past labour are still surrounded by such comforts and luxuries as they have been accustomed to. In all this world such a thing as poverty is unknown. Nor can anyone become rich. No matter how much a man or woman may spare the State account, he or she can hoard nothing, nor even draw upon the depot for articles that must run to waste. Nor can anyone own a foot of land. No one can make a will. At death, or prior to that event, purely personal belongings may be promised or given to various members of a family, but there can be no bickering over the distribution of wealth. The State is the heir of each generation, and as the lives of all our men and women are honourable and profitable, as we have no criminals and no paupers, and as all work who are permitted to do so, the State gains much by each generation, and can easily afford to sustain teachers and the like, maintain schools and places of amusement in each centre of population, and provide for the wants of worn-out workers.

'And our workers do not wear out soon. The conditions of life are easy and they are free from worry and almost free from temptation. Our day is twenty-five hours and they only work five at a trade. The majority work a little in the afternoons in their fruit and flower gardens or for their own amusement, but there is no such thing as bustle, strain, anxiety as to money or any other worrying matter. The general happiness and the zest manifested by comparatively aged people doubtless has its source in the conditions of life.

'Our intercourse with one another is very easy. We are not expected to provide foods and drinks for our afternoon or evening guests. Those who wish to eat together go to the caravansary, where wholesome and varied meats are supplied early in the afternoon to all comers, the only formality being that each name is sent to the depot for the district. You pay for your friend's dinner if you wish by repeating your own name. This, however, is rarely allowed, for your friend is your equal, and stands as well in the register as you do.

'Another reason for the freedom of our intercourse is freedom from titles. We have no "Miss" nor "Mistress", no "Sir" nor "Esquire". Each man or woman goes by name. The profession is allowed to be used as an affix, as "Class-mother", "Doctor", "Teacher", but even these confer no rank.

'I did not gather up all the above information while out skating with Father. I got most of it at various times from Gaston, who spends half-an-hour every fourth day in telling us of things pertaining to our everyday lives. I am getting on well with my studies. It is very easy to learn, every study is made so interesting. We were prepared for Gaston's class while going through Hildreth's, and the present teacher seems to know just what we want to learn next. We do not appear to have much to learn in ordinary arithmetic, and we are busy measuring surfaces and solids of various forms every morning. When we have proved by our arithmetic that a certain surface contains a certain number of feet, we have to measure it up in single feet and show them. For this we have a large ground space that will bear chalking and a smooth, black wall in the playground. Sometimes several pupils join in working out a problem in full size. The other day I and two classmates had to find the centre of a polygon – an irregular one. We worked at it for two hours, making triangles and measuring their area and finding the centres, first of one, then of two, until at last we got the centre of all the centres.

'The next day we had to work it out again on a small scale on thin cardboard. When this was done the figure was cut out and balanced on a point, and in two cases out of three the centre had been so correctly found that the balancing point coincided with the centres we had discovered. The third was very nearly correct. All our lessons were made interesting in this way, and when we had learned them we could not forget them.

'In order to learn geography we had to find the cardinal points by the sun, and to draw plans of the school, the playfields, paths and environs. Then we were led on to draw more extended plans on a smaller scale, including the positions of scores of houses and in each case showing the way to the pupil's own abode.

'Until we were well versed in topography we were taught nothing of geography. The former science was merged into the latter one. We were well advanced in the study of geography before we knew that we had begun it. Gaston teaches us what is called the "ancient" system, a division that was in vogue many thousands of years ago, when we had many nations and different languages and political systems. This system gives us historic names, and has something of poetry and suggestiveness in it, especially for the people who rejoice in having descended from the grander of the old nations. The new system of districts and sections, bounded only by the invisible lines of latitude and longitude, and distinguished mostly by numbers, may be more practical and handier for telegraphic and other modes of communication, but it has none of the charms of association with a past out of which we have gradually emerged.

'There is no political geography to study, for we have only one government, which Gaston calls an Executive. It has to watch the whole planet for the benefit of all the people, to prevent excesses and deficiencies of manufacture and production, to store up surpluses and send supplies to any district that is likely to suffer from scarcity. It regulates the great streams of what at one time would have been called commerce.

'In teaching geography Gaston uses a great globe so mounted that we can all see it. Our world has two great oceans and several smaller seas surrounded by land. The water surface is about one third, the land surface two thirds, of the whole. Gaston tells us of thousands of miles of canals[8] connecting these oceans, and of thousands of ships that are used in carrying heavy and bulky articles from place to place by these oceans, seas and canals. He says that on some planets there is a much larger area covered with water. Our nearest neighbour, and nearer to the sun, a larger planet than ours, having mostly two great masses of land surrounded by water and being about two-thirds covered with water. This planet is much studied and constantly watched with most powerful telescopes, for it is known to be inhabited by rational beings. Proofs of this are given by some of the giant telescopes, and there are other sources of information.

---

8 This mention of canals likely derives from the Italian astronomer
   Schiaparelli's 1877 observations of 'canali' (or 'channels') on Mars. These
   became 'canals' in English translation, gaining the implication of being
   intentionally built. Parrinder explains that in 1909, the observatory in
   Mount Wilson, California, captured data that revealed the canals to be
   canyons that resulted from erosion. Patrick Parrinder, *Utopian Literature
   and Science: From the Scientific Revolution to Brave New World and Beyond*
   (New York: Palgrave Macmillan, 2015), 30–32.

'Gaston teaches us how to draw globes and maps, and to put in the proper lines of longitude and latitude, but his course does not include astronomical geography. Not that we are left in entire ignorance even of that branch, for Gaston made the room dark on several fourth days, and spent his half hour in showing by globes of light and the big globe how days and nights came, and how we got winter and summer, and why some parts of the world were hotter than others, and how by going in one direction or another we lost sight of certain stars and stood at different angles to the sunlight.

'He taught us a good deal regarding our two moons, the near one that flies round the world more than three times a day, and the other that takes more than a day to get through its changes. These moons are of very little use as givers of light, but the nearer one keeps the air in motion in equatorial regions, and by causing a small, swift-moving tide does the same thing for the central seas. Exact details of these subjects he did not give – what he told us just sharpened up our appetites for more knowledge.

'I have learned to skate easily without tumbling, and I find that Mother can skate just as well as any of us, if not better. She and Father sometimes leave me to take care of Emma, who is too little yet, and away they go gliding as merrily as the rest. Mother is the merriest and prettiest woman of them all.

'Our time in Gaston's class is nearly over. It is and has been a happy time for all concerned. There has been no inattention and there is not a boy in the class, nor a girl either, who has fallen short of the expectations of the teacher. We have not a single dunce. We have all had our education carried far enough to enable us to travel to any part of the world and engage in any ordinary industrial pursuit. When I leave I have to help Mother at home for about half a year and learn how to perform domestic duties, and then to go to the school of mechanics and learn to make electrical machinery like Father does.'

This chapter contains a condensed statement of all that our diarist has written during nearly two years. He has evidently got to seeing more clearly and knowing more in his dream-life. His mental growth is apparently rapid, but not more so than that of his peers. Evidently the children with whom he is associated are clever, intelligent and morally better than the average whom he would meet in any school on Earth. Possibly the civilisation of the planet upon which he lives much of his time, the planet Mars, is much older and much higher than that of the Earth. The people appear to have nothing to worry them, no monetary difficulties, no strife nor unhealthy competition, no contending nationalities, no wars, no crimes. Naturally, being introduced to such people, we want to know more of them, their modes of life, their history, how their lives came to be so fully perfected. Fortunately, our diarist has much to tell upon these points, and his teachers, finding out that he is living a dual life, give him several standards of comparison that enable him to compare measurements and enable us to understand Martial humanity.

CHAPTER VII

Bertrand's School of Mechanics

'For four days, the working week in all our world, we have been going to Bertrand's school, not to take any lessons, but to see it all and get acquainted with its many wonders. There are about twenty classroom workshops, each adapted to the requirements of one hundred pupils. There are fifty working benches, one for each pair of co-workers. All the tools required for each kind of work are placed in racks within easy reach of the hands using them, and they are all the best of their kind. Wherever running machinery is used, power is supplied from a great central engine driven by electricity. The first floor over the workshops contains thousands of models of the best machines in existence for the performance of the various kinds of work that have to be done. Each model is complete in all parts, and can actually do on a small scale the work for which it is intended. These models are not merely intended to stand in cases, but to be freely used by teachers and pupils in the prosecution of their studies. On the first floor there is also a lecture hall, where all the pupils are assembled once a week to receive instruction

from one of the masters or from some travelling special-
ist. The second floor contains classrooms corresponding
with the lower ones. These are used by the pupils for the
prosecution of their theoretical studies, drawing of plans,
mathematics and the like. On the great, flat roof there
were models of all the kinds of machinery driven by wind,
and instruments for meteorological purposes.

'For four days the great school was open to all who chose
to visit it, and the more advanced pupils explained the
uses of instruments and machines, and worked hundreds
of the models for the benefit of the new pupils and the
instruction of people whose studies and labours had been
expended in other directions. At the end of the time there
was not a machine out of place, not an article damaged or
missing. There are no locks on the school doors; in fact,
when I come to think of it, I cannot remember having
seen a lock or bar anywhere.

'On the following first day, the school was opened for
a new annual session, to consist of five hundred working
days of five hours each.

'The morning was spent in placing the new pupils
and preliminary work, and for the last hour we were assembled in the main hall to hear the inaugural address of
Headmaster Bertrand.

'He chose for his subject electricity.

'Nothing could have pleased me better, for Gaston had
made the subject interesting, and Father had taught me
that to this power we were indebted for the motion of our
air boat and sleigh, for our fire and light.

'To give more than a brief account of Bertrand's address
is impossible; to illustrate and explain his experiments
alone would require a volume. He made his spoken words

into raised signs on sheets of metal, so that a blind man knowing our electrical signs might have read them by touch. He caused us to hear laughter, speech and song that were produced a thousand miles away, and he let us hear the living voices of great men and women who had been dead to us for a thousand years. He concentrated heat so that he could melt steel in a few minutes; he caused his dynamos to give off a gentle warmth that would keep a room at a certain temperature, or that would just simmer some article of food without making it boil. He concentrated light and diffused it, threw heat rays to a distance and lit inflammable substances. He put an electric wire round a log of wood eighteen inches in diameter and cut through it in a few seconds. He allowed us surgical instruments that could be made to perform operations with incredible speed. He decomposed water and made water from the air around us. He performed feats in chemistry with the aid of what appeared to be a plaything in his hands. At a signal from the lecturer the room was instantly darkened, and now commenced a series of wonderful displays: the Aurora Borealis, the rainbow, the primary colours, the lines telling of what substances were being consumed or heated behind the lights given forth, the polarisation and depolarisation of light, photography. All these came and went with amazing swiftness. It took me many months to understand a tithe of what he did with electricity, and yet I found that he had not mentioned a tithe of the uses to which it is put upon our planet.

'Bertrand claimed for electricity something more than a first place amongst the forces of nature. Said he: "We have not to regard wind as one force, water as another, heat and light as two more forces. We have rather to regard electricity as the one great force, and all the rest of the so-called forces of nature as various manifestations of and modifications of that one force.

"The sun is the central dynamo of our system. All the positive forms of electricity come from him. The pull and the push of the positive and negative forms cause rotation and orbital movement in the planets. There is no such force as gravitation: the planets are held in their respective relationship to each other and to the central sun, the satellites to their planets, our sun to his neighbours, and the stellar systems to each other by a force that acts instantaneously and simultaneously in all parts. That force is electricity. From a distance great enough, what we call the universe appears as a solid gem; electricity is the force that welds the ten billion suns into that solid.

"Ever since human life began to be civilised, men have been trying to harness the various forms of force. The winds, falling water, steam, have all in turn played their part, and are still used in some places and for some purpose. I have no need to show how each of these are merely protean forms of the same face.

"For several thousands of years we used these as our motive powers, and our world grew civilised and populous during this period. For some hundreds of years in the latter part of this time, we used electricity. First it was a plaything of scientists, and then it began to be used as a messenger over the lands and under the seas. It was not long before we found that it could be made to carry and record sounds, and we could hear the voices of the long-since departed. At this time, it came into use as an illuminator, and the world became brilliant with the electric light.

"Invention succeeded invention until steam was superseded as a motive power, and electricity had taken its place on sea and on land. To provide electricity, winds, tides, falling waters and melting snows were all laid under contribution, and force was often carried by wire and used hundreds of miles from where it was generated. On the great plains where water had but little fall, and where the winds could not be relied upon, steam was used to generate electric force in great dynamos. This tended to rapidly use up all our combustible minerals, all surface combustibles having been used up long before. Peat, brown coal, lignite, oil shale, hard coal, bitumen, and such soft limestone as would burn with other substances but not alone got used up in turn, and our vast population of three-thousand million people were brought face to face with one of the greatest problems that ever a mass of human beings were called upon to solve; viz., how to generate heat to cook their food, and keep themselves alive on the surface of a cool planet without the aid of combustible materials.

"A great inventor found out the method of releasing electrical force in slower vibrations, so that heat instead of light was produced; but at first there was little gain in this transaction, for the electricity itself had frequently to be produced by steam power. The gain was more apparent when wind and water were utilised. Millions of people felt relief when they could make their light into a fire hot enough to cook with, or into a non-radiant warmth that made the winter temperature of their rooms something like pleasant.

"There were still great districts in the north and south where neither fuel nor water power were available, and the inhabitants were put to sore straits. Those who could left their homes and spent the winter in tropical regions, but the whole population could not migrate. In some instances a community would take possession of a dry cavern, store it with provisions, and spend the colder months of the winter out of the reach of frost and snow. Our planet, as you are aware, is peculiarly rich in caverns, owing to shrinkage of its surface rocks.

"In some regions exposed to cold now and then, but not perpetually covered with snow nor exposed to frost (the milder portions of the temperate zones in the north and south), free use was made of hand dynamos. When the housewife wanted a fire, someone had to work vigorously in turning a wheel, the muscular force of a man being transformed into electrical force and released as fire. In these regions, chemical electricity was used as a weak lighting power. Asses sometimes worked all day charging accumulators, and when a wind blew there were thousands of sails to catch it. In spite of all that could be done, however, human life could not be supported beyond the fiftieth parallels of latitude north and south. This caused an over crowding of the temperate and tropical regions, and made the struggle for existence very intense. The food-producing area became too small, and the means of sustaining life fully could only be gained by those of strong hand and superior brain. Millions of the weaker men and women had their lives shortened by semi-starvation, and millions more died of diseases caused by cold. The people lost courage; the marriage rate decreased very much; the death rate increased continually; the birth rate decreased; and during a single century the population fell off to the extent of one-sixth. That is, at the end of the century we were fewer by five hundred million than at the beginning. Going on at this rate we should soon have had a small population living in the equatorial regions, and no more. Although we have had a hundred happy and prosperous centuries since that doleful time, that century is still remembered as the 'Black Century'.

"We now come to the greatest discovery ever made upon this planet.

"It was made by accident.

"Most of you know more or less of it, and we all benefit by it, and our posterity to the end of time will continue to do so.

"You know that several of the caverns in the north go to a great depth, and that some of them extend scores of miles underground; that in some there are lakes and rivers and vast spaces in which the air is pure and never falls below a comfortable temperature.

"In one of these somewhere, about one hundred thousand people had prepared their winter abode. Bedding, warm clothing, food, and as many necessaries as could be transferred from the homes for a score of miles round had been carried into the silent depths of one of these great caves. The people, bound together by a common difficulty, made their burdens lighter by sharing them. The strong helped the weak; those who had plenty shared with the sick, the needy and the aged. We had already reached a high stage of civilisation, and life generally had become altruistic. No one lived for self alone, or sought to profit by the loss of another.

"From the entrance of this cavern to the bottom of it was a steep descent of about twelve miles. Ropes and stairways had been provided in the difficult parts, but it still remained a toilsome task to go to the surface and back again. Women and children generally remained down about one hundred to one hundred and thirty days, according to the length and severity of the winter. A deep, clear stream in the bottom of the cave supplied water. Great care was taken so that the water should not become polluted. The supply of air was perfect.

"Scarcely had the community got settled when they began to notice that their water was turbid at times, that it was sometimes warmer than common, and that some days there was no water to be had except what could be caught from the roof of some caverns that were too damp to be habitable. It was soon decided by those in authority to follow the water by boring, and the requisite machinery was quickly got to work.

"The floor of the cave is five miles in vertical depth from the surface, so the people thought they could not have to go far before getting to water. In this they were disappointed. The bore was tubed for nearly two miles, and it was finally decided to work one more day and give up. How little the workers thought that the destiny of a world hung upon that decision. What would our race's life have been by this time if those men had not decided to work one day more?

"Barely had the machine begun to work on the morning of this last day when the great cave became a blaze of light that was brighter by far than the day on the surface above the cave. What had happened? A crowd of people rushed towards the light from all sides. They met several others coming from it; some of them were carrying wounded men. Close by the light were two objects that could only be viewed with a shudder. They were a pair of blackened cinders, shrivelled up into half their original size. The electric fire that had leaped up the rod and tubes of the bore had rushed through these two bodies, and not only killed but cremated them before they had time to fall to the ground.

"What about the water? There was none where that fire came from, but by some strange connection of the two events, or perhaps by some coincidence, the stream began to flow again, and the lake filled up to its old level.

"Two men were killed, one died next day, the rest recovered. The people in the cave had water in abundance, and a source of great light that changed its colours now and then but never diminished. And now the questions arose, what is the light? Whence comes it? Is it likely to be permanent?

"A great electrician was sent for, and with him came a geologist and some other specialists. After a series of experiments, they came to the conclusion that the outer flow of electricity – that which goes back to the southern electric pole, following lines not far below the surface of the planet – had been tapped, and that the light was electric. The flow from that source would not be likely to cease unless it was a temporary current following some flaw in the rock and tending to produce volcanic action.

"The next work was conducting the electricity in manageable quantities along wires to the surface. Before the following winter this was done, and as a result there was no need for the usual migration, for every home and every schoolhouse or other public building was adequately warmed and lighted.

"Since then, the source of electric power had been tapped in more than a thousand places, and as you know almost all the world's work is done by power drawn from beneath its surface rocks. You cannot go twenty miles in any direction without finding an electric fountain, free to the public, from which the accumulators of any travelling machine can be instantly recharged.

"We cannot use up this force. The source of heat and light will remain until the sun himself grows cold and dark. Each planet is a great electrical machine. If you strip off its outer coverings as you would peel an orange, you come to where the ball is wrapped in currents running from north to south; and, if you could live far beneath the surface at the south magnetic pole, you would see those millions of currents pouring into one that returns through the core of the globe from pole to pole. If any planet could lose a share of its magnetic life, it would be instantly re-supplied from the sun. We, however, cannot consume any of this force. We only detain it and make it work for us on its way. It does not feel the work it does for us any more than the sun feels the effort by which it raises vapor into the air and piles snow upon the mountain top.

"Monuments of those who perished that eventful day have been made in solid silver and can be seen in the Central Museum. Let us hope that they know of the great boon that came into human life when they were so suddenly hurled out of it."

'For several days Bertrand's address formed a theme for conversation. Some said that he had received instructions from the Planetary Executive to direct as many youths as possible to prepare themselves for the work of making electrical machinery, the demand for such being greater than the supply. If that were the case, he had certainly adopted the best measures possible, for quite one half of our pupils went into the workshops where such machinery is made, and many more became designers and inventors.'

There is no need to follow our schoolboy diarist through his third educational course. Nothing very startling or sensational occurs. He has a few accidents, and sometimes takes an electric shock that makes him feel for a while as if his limbs were all dislocated. Any of these would have killed him in a real workshop, but sufficient power is not allowed to students, else few would get through their technical course.

He forms some valuable friendships, and at the end of the term goes into a great manufactory of electric motors. These are in great demand. They are let by the Government to those who need them in the preparation of produce, in manufacture or for pleasure. They are made by the government, and do not belong to private individuals. Those who use them, it appears, have the rent charge debited in their private account.

About the end of his five-hundred-day term at the technical school our diarist writes: 'I have passed the final examinations with flying colours. As a student of the theoretical branches, I was very eager. I desired to master the mathematical sides of the electrical problem as well as the mechanical ones. I plainly saw that very low rates of vibration would produce sound, that higher rates would give power in higher and still higher grades of intensity; that higher rates would give chemical action and still more rapid would give heat in a diffused gentle form; increase the rate of vibration still more and we reach the point where red heat gives off the first rays of red light. From this point to the extreme violet, light is again only a series of changes in rate of vibration.

'In these light vibrations I was not particularly interested, but I saw that even yet there was much to be discovered regarding the effects producible by electricity in the various states and rates of motion between the highest sound vibration and the lowest of the heat and light series. It appeared to me that if these rates could be utilised they might – by acting on the soil, the water and the air – increase productiveness, there being no need to hesitate in drawing upon an illimitable supply of force.

'I had read a deal about the time following upon the "Black Century", and of the marvels wrought by the new source of power. I had seen that the introduction of abundant heat, light and power had so stimulated industry and production that life had become easy and the means of sustaining it had become abundant, with the result that the population doubled in a little more than a century. In the "Black Century" we lost five hundred million, yet before the conclusion of the second century our population had almost reached its present number of over five thousand million – enormous for the size of our planet.

'My idea was, and is still, that further knowledge in chemical vibrations will double or treble the productiveness of the soil, and both reduce the labour of the agriculturist and increase indefinitely the amount of his productions. Why may we not have two harvests in place of one? Why may we not get chemically from air, water and earth the foods that plants combine in their organised structures?

'I left Bertrand's school full of new ideas and quite ready to commence learning my trade, but my father was fully determined that I should spend half a year at home and visit the Central Museum in his company for a week or two. To this I fully agreed, especially as another spring was already here, and I might make one or two preliminary experiments on a small scale.'

CHAPTER VIII

MY DISCOVERY

'I HAVE NOT previously mentioned in these diaries the fact that electricity is supplied free to everyone who uses it on our planet. There is no attempt to measure the consumption and no stint placed on its use. For the supply is inexhaustible, and even the use does not diminish force; it merely makes it serve our purpose in passing. When we release the electricity it just runs back into the down current, and may be in our hands again in a few seconds later.

'There was, therefore, no difficulty in getting a wire laid into a carefully prepared garden plot. In this I had planted a few common vegetables. I passed the current through a regulator and then laid coils all over the plot just beneath the soil. My object was to raise the temperature of the soil a little higher than that of the surrounding air, and to keep it night and day in the same condition.

'I had another plot of the same size planted in a similar manner and fertilised with the same ingredients. In ninety days the plants had attained the ordinary maturity, but I allowed them to remain thirty days more and they reached quite double size. The crop sown in the same way, and grown in the ordinary way, was as far advanced in one hundred and eighty days as the other in ninety. On analysing the soil from the two plots, I found that the quicker growing and bulkier plants had taken little, if any, more out of the soil than the ordinary plants had absorbed. I therefore came to the conclusion that the gentle stimulus of a little warmth in the soil had caused a more rapid absorption of water and atmospheric constituents.

'We, Father and I, sent an account of our discovery to the Minister of Agriculture in the Planetary Executive. He advised further and more extended experiments. He said we must find out if the extra crop paid the extra cost in labour and material involved by the laying of wires and attention; that we must have the bulkier productions analysed to see if their nourishing qualities were increased in proportion to their increased bulk, for there would be no gain in causing a plant to swell by the absorption of fluid.

'We made the experiments as advised. We found that the invention could be advantageously utilised if the wires were laid in tubes at a depth of from twelve to fourteen inches and made a permanent fixture; that the best results were produced by turning on the electricity at nightfall; that pound for pound the new plants were as good as the old ones; that it would not pay to run the wires into the soil each time the ground was planted.

'All our experiments were submitted to experts appointed by the Minister of Agriculture, and when at the conclusion they were pronounced satisfactory, my father and I each received the Order of Freedom, the outer insignia of which is a badge and a gold medal, and the meaning of which is significant: wearers are free to visit all workshops, mines and places of interest in any part; to work when and where we choose, and to call on anyone to assist in making experiments, removing plant and, in short, doing anything to assist in furthering useful projects; to travel by underground lines, by canals, by sea or by air boat just when we please and as far as we choose; to make use of any hostel or caravansary as long as we like. In short, to have no expenses charged to our debit, to have all that the planet can afford as free as air.

'We cannot have a patent right, cannot sell our invention, cannot give it any monetary value; but when once recognised as of great public utility, an inventor (or signal benefactor of humanity) receives this order, which practically places all the resources of a civilisation that has been growing for one hundred thousand years at his disposal. What millionaire could have so much?

'The wearer of this badge has no account to render of his work. He might retire from active pursuits for the remainder of his days, and pass the time enjoying himself and travelling at will, for the privilege extends to his wife and family. But this has never been known to happen: the men who have the Freedom are generally active and enterprising, and by their labours the most profitable members of the human family. For my own part, as I am only just over eight years of age, I will spend a year in learning to make electrical machinery. Five hundred days is reckoned a working year. Our actual year is six hundred and eighty-seven days of twenty-five hours each. Of these, each fifth day is a rest day, our Sabbath, but not wholly devoted to public worship. This leaves us five hundred and forty-nine working days. Of these, five hundred are claimed for work, the odd days are used for travelling and recreation, if you see fit. Married men will generally take their families for an outing twice a year. The working hours of a day are five, and even these could be reduced, for owing to the great skill of our highly trained population, and to the extensive use of machinery and the unlimited electrical power at our disposal, our productions are so abundant in all directions that every person on the planet is supplied, and we have orders at times to cease producing and manufacturing for a while.

'We have no armies, no police, no aristocracy of a non-productive kind and no middle men to live on the labours of the producer by the processes of buying, selling and making a profit. Thus it comes to pass that everyone has all needs supplied, and out of the general abundance has many luxuries.

'Another reason for the general abundance is that no one wastes or wantonly destroys anything; nor does anyone wear or use anything for purposes of ostentation or display. All this is useless in a land where there is no personal wealth, and no means of using riches if specially possessed. All who can work do so for the general good, and working five hours daily causes a rate of production much in advance of consumption. The probability is that the hours of labour will have to be reduced to four, or even three. This would have come about long since had not many millions of men been employed on public works for centuries.

'All our magnificent railways are carried underground on wide, well-ventilated, brilliantly lighted roads. This had to be done in order that the land occupied by them might be used for agriculture. Of our rainfall, none is wasted. It is stored in thousands of reservoirs, and utilised for irrigation in dry seasons. The failure of a crop would be such a terrible disaster that we provide for it by building and filling immense storehouses, with all stores being so preserved and sealed as to ensure their sweetness and nutritive qualities whenever they may be required. These and a thousand other public works, efforts that have made our whole planet a smiling and fertile thing of beauty, have absorbed a vast amount of labour. As it is, each worker follows his occupation about one-seventh of his time, and the number of workers engaged in productive and manufacturing industries are about one-eighth of the population.

'One man, tilling the soil, can grow food for fifty; another, weaving cloth, can dress three hundred and four men; one, making boots or hats, can cover the extremities of a thousand fellow mortals. Hence it comes that we have to work so little and are yet so well supplied.

'Tomorrow I begin the ninth year of my life, and the first day of my five hundred days of self-imposed mechanical training. When this year is finished I will travel, and, working in various parts, perfect my education.'

This brief chapter covers about three years of our diarist's records. By Earth-time he is a little over seventeen years of age; by that of Mars he has finished his eighth year. All that is of any importance to the narrative and much of what he has learned of the actual life of the Martial humans is included in the chapter.

CHAPTER IX

My Use of the Freedom

'FROM NOW FORWARD, as long as I live, I can draw from any depot on the planet anything that I want. I can visit any workshop or mine; can travel by any public conveyance; can work at any trade; can study any subject at any seat of learning; can use to any extent telegraphic, telephonic or other means of communication; can see the most sacred and ancient manuscripts and books of the ages that are gone; can visit the observatories, of which we have many, and study the heavens by the aid of the most powerful telescopes to be found in the universe. I can dress as I please, and wherever my lot is cast, the best of accommodation and provision is at my service. When I marry, if ever such an event should occur, my wife will have the same advantages. Seeing that such a favour has at this early period of my life been conferred upon me, I will take care to be worthy of it. Already I can see many ways in which my discovery can be utilised. If I make myself thoroughly capable as a mechanic, I shall be able to do much more than I can now. Still, no pupil who has gone through a course at Bertrand's technical school can complain of inability to use tools and understand mechanical operations, and his school is only one of thousands of similar ones.

'I have not said much of our sports and games, but it must not be inferred that we have no play. Indeed, I question if there is any place in the solar system, at any rate, where we can be beaten in the enjoyment of active sports and games. Public gymnasiums are very abundant, and men and women of all ages visit them. For a few years after she is married, a woman has probably other duties to attend to and does not frequent the gymnasiums, but she comes with her sons and daughters in a while, and lets them see that the skill and strength of her youth have not quite departed. Probably we owe much of our activity, vigour, health and longevity to this kind of education. If we did not play we should not develop our muscles and become the well-knit and compact people that we are. For our work is so easy and light that it would not alone cause more than a very partial development. We have ball games of more than a dozen kinds; we have skating and ice dances, sleighing, sliding, hill shooting with small sleighs, upon which only two people can sit. We have dancing and archery and music – music to everything and everywhere. We have air sports. Sometimes a hundred flying fishes will take turns at performing difficult feats. These are generally little air boats built for the use of one person, though larger ones are sometimes brought into play. People are not allowed to use air boats until they have had plenty of practice in rapid movements, executed with great precision.

'The swift descent is always one part of a programme of air sports. Twenty boats or so are placed in line, forty feet apart, so that their wings will not be liable to clash, at the height of a thousand feet. At a given signal an article is dropped from each, and each boat darts down in pursuit. The boat has to pass the falling body, and to go underneath and catch it. In a competition of this kind more than half will succeed, and first place is given to the one who catches his falling body the first and commences remounting. The successful competitors are placed in line again at a height of six hundred feet, and again at three hundred feet, until the most skillful sailor is discovered.

'I take my share in these air sports and have proved myself competent, thanks to Father, who, for months, patiently instructed me and superintended my practice. I took great interest in air sailing, for did I not owe my life to Father's skill in this very art?

'A balloon hunt is another feature of our air sports. A small balloon is inflated and allowed to ascend for about a mile in vertical height, during which time it may have drifted a good distance. When it is supposed to be high enough and far enough away to endure a good chase, a number of competitors start in pursuit. It is understood that when the racers see that one of their number is in reach that they cease flying, lest the boats collide. This rule is usually obeyed; indeed, we have no willful lawbreakers anywhere.

'On the occasion of my last balloon hunt, however, I had succeeded in reaching the prize a little in advance of my friends, and had just seized the cord to open the valve, which would have emptied the balloon in two minutes, when crash goes the left wing of my boat, and over it tilts, pitching me from my seat. Fortunately, my first instinct led me to clutch the little ring of cords attached to the mouth of my prize, and so when my disabled boat sank from under me, I was hanging by my hands to the balloon. This was not large enough to sustain my weight, and so I began to follow my boat. The man who had drifted against me and caused my accident kept close, so that he could aid me at any moment. We got to the ground in safety; I alighted no more heavily than if I had jumped from a height of six feet. Several of my friends followed my boat, and staying the rapidity of its descent, got it to the ground without further damage. Such presence of mind is very common. It is largely used in averting accidents on sea, on land and in the air.

'Although we are not great travellers by water, and in spite of rivers and seas being scarce, those of us who have the opportunity make the most of aquatic sports. We all learn to swim, and sailing and rowing are very common accomplishments. We dive at great depths also, and we keep our seas clear of the enemies of the edible fish. We do not care to have sea monsters robbing us of an important article of food, nor have them make bathing and swim-ming dangerous pastimes. We do a great deal of fishing, both in fresh and salt water. Our sea water is very cold, and so dense with salt and dissolved mineral matters that we can scarcely sink in it.

'We have no hunting of wild beasts; they have all been exterminated long ago. This extermination has extended to vermin and insect plagues, and even to some kinds of animalculæ[9]. There is nothing that can bite, sting or injure us in any way.

9 Animalculæ here refers to small animals, including single-celled organisms, insects, invertebrates, and small sea life.

We have done for the air what we have done for the sea. Our birds of song have not to dread the hawk, and our plumper edible birds have nothing to fear unless they get too numerous, in which case they are killed by the silent discharge of an electric fowling piece. We have no large cattle nor any horses, only asses and goats. A few playful, half-tame little animals are to be seen in forest reserves, but these do not trench upon food supplies, nor take up ground that could be devoted to farming.

'Gunnery is almost a lost art, partly because men have ceased to slay each other and partly because there is nothing to destroy. Still we practise archery pretty freely, for both sexes can join in the game and it is not a wasteful pastime. Our ammunition serves again and again; indeed, our metals are none too abundant. We have none to waste in useless tools, and none to fire away in balls, bullets and shot. We have plenty of games for either sex, and plenty in which both can participate, but we have not one that of necessity involves waste or is uncommonly dangerous to life or limb. We have accidents now and then, whether at work or at play, and sometimes deaths occur, but these do not furnish reasons for giving up our games.'

Such is the gist of our diarist's communications during nearly two years. He says a great deal about the workshop, the work and the thoughtful and skilful men who instruct him from time to time. He even repeats many little scraps of conversation, and tells of incidents in home-life and that of the workshop, but if the diary were copied in its entirety there would be little to interest the general reader. He now says that he is going to commence his tenth year and his travels about at the same time.

CHAPTER X

My Journeyings

'MOTHER KNOWS THE world better than I do; knows that wherever I go everything I can want and need will be placed at my disposal, and yet she wants me to take several things with me; to pack a box and carry changes of clothing and some personal belongings, which she says I may not always be able to get. I thought of only taking my haversack in which to carry my notebooks and so forth, but I must obey my mother. After all, a box needs not be much of an encumbrance. If I have to walk sometimes and at others to fly where luggage is not carried, I can get the box sent on to meet me at any suitable point.

'Father is not going with me, but will come and spend a while with me in the capital. Mother and my sister Emma, who is as tall as Mother, and well educated and accomplished as a musician and artist, will probably accompany him.

'For me there are several modes of travel from which I can choose. From the nearest depot I can get an air boat and fly with it as long as I require it, leaving it at the nearest depot when done with. If I take it the whole fifteen thousand miles, it will be just as much a chattel of the Government and just as much at home as now. Its use for the time I have had it will be debited to me, that is all. I am under no obligation to return it. If articles get congested in one place they are redistributed; but this rarely happens. My freedom causes the depot to debit the Government, for they have to give an account to the Central.

'I do not take an air boat, for the weather is cold and the mode of travel lonely. Besides, in flying, eternal vigilance has to be manifested and occasional descents made to resupply electricity. We carry a chemical generator for an emergency, such as being caught in mid air with no means of controlling descent, and so having to fall. In some places supply wires are thirty miles apart. It is possible to pass one and be unable to reach another; it is therefore necessary to know how far you can go and how far you have gone.

'Another mode is by the swift air boats that carry despatches and special messengers. These go through the upper air, above the level of ordinary traffic, at an average speed of one hundred miles an hour; on emergency they go at twice the speed. Even that is slow compared with the rate of a dozen centuries ago, at which period everything used to go in a greater hurry. It was discovered, however, that the rapidity of travel made drivers nervous, and materially impaired their health and shortened their lives. A parliament was convened and the question of rates of travel fully discussed. The result is we travel slower and live longer. It is a matter of history that one of the Government air boats, about twelve hundred years ago, went round the planet in four days. That is, it travelled over three hundred miles an hour.

'I decided not to go by the Government boat. My medal would pass me, but my journey to the metropolis was not of State importance, and to have used the boat would have been to tax my prerogative to the utmost. Fifteen thousand miles is a long journey in any case.

'Two more ways lay open; by rail, skirting the south of the Central Ocean, and by rail and sea, taking a warmer and more northerly route. The latter I selected.

'Our lines all run underground, so that travellers by rail see nothing of the country, and have no night or day. The propelling force is the usual one. The cars are well lit and supplied with every convenience. In them you can eat, drink, sleep, read, bathe, work and write; in short, make yourself at home. The maximum rate of travel is one hundred miles an hour, and the cars are suspended between the wheels, so that motion is scarcely felt. The sound also is deadened so much that ordinary conversation is heard as if in a drawing room. In winter, railway travelling is the most comfortable, for one thing the warmest.

'As we have no waste spaces, and depots for the reception and distribution of produce have not to be far apart, we have need for a vast railway system. Heavy goods of all kinds are carried underground. Articles are rarely consumed in any quantity where they are produced. This causes a great amount of traffic. Trains are run very frequently. We have branch lines and perfect communication with every district. They do not run from city to city, because we have no cities in the ordinary sense of the term. In no part have we buildings massed together, no streets, and no dense masses of population. Where manufactures are carried on, houses are nearer together; in agricultural areas they are further apart, but they never touch one another. The number of railway stations is regulated by the density of the population of the district, and there is always a station near a depot for the reception and distribution of commodities.

'During my first day's travel, nothing occurred that requires mention; but early on the second day a traveller joined me whom I cannot forget in a hurry. He was an old man, very old, one who would appear aged amongst people who are in the habit of growing old. Our people almost always die of old age, and yet, all the old men I have seen appear young when compared with this man.

'His hair was a soft white fleece of silvery whiteness and beautiful to look upon; his full beard, reaching down to his waist and of the same whiteness, gave him a peculiarly venerable appearance. I have never seen a face like his. The skin had in it literally thousands of finely traced wrinkles and was semi-transparent. It appeared as if a faint light glowed beneath it; the features were very fine and harmonious; indeed, he had the peculiar beauty, which belongs to the old age of a remarkably good life. Old as he was, he presented no sign of senility; he was active in his movements, and every sense and faculty appeared to be on the alert.

'When I saw that the old man intended to get into the train, I went to his assistance and carried a handbag for him. We went into one of the cosy sitting rooms and got into conversation. He saw that I wore the Badge of Freedom, which he also carried, and asked me how I had obtained that honour at such an early period of my youth. His views regarding the use of the badge were entirely in harmony with my own. He had gained the honour by mathematical and astronomical research.

'We exchanged cards, and finding that we were bound to the same place, to the intellectual centre of the metropolis, we decided to travel together. I say the "centre" of the metropolis because the metropolitan area is a thousand miles long and five hundred in width; it contains one-fifth of the population of the planet. But even here, each house has about a rood of land, and fruits and vegetables are grown in great abundance; the whole area is more like a park than a city, so says my new friend.

'As we conversed on general topics, I perceived that my new friend regarded me with closer and closer attention, and after a while he appeared to recall something to mind: "Charles Frankston," says he. "Charles Frankston," again, as if speaking to himself.

"Did you not have a fall from your father's air boat when you were a little boy?"

"I did, and can remember the sensation to this day."

"And you were unconscious for some time, several days?"

"Yes; about ten days."

"You were attended by Doctor Hildreth?"

"I was; she is still the medical officer of our district."

"Do you remember anything of that time, any peculiar experiences, strange thoughts or dreams?"

"No; but I overheard a conversation in which it was said that I was an Earthborn and still living on that planet."

"Will you allow me to find out if that is correct?"

"Yes, if you can do so. I am entirely unconscious of anything of the kind, though my mother says that I have put questions that indicate some experiences or thoughts that I cannot have had during my present existence."

"Can you trust me to deprive you of your consciousness for a few moments? I will do you no harm."

"Certainly I can. I feel that I may trust you with anything, even my present or eternal welfare."

"Fix your eyes; look steadily into mine."

'I obeyed. In a few moments his eyes appeared to merge into one large brilliant eye, and his white head and beard became a mighty mass blocking up half my sky.

'Suddenly, I lost sight of both eye and head, and attained a new and strange consciousness. I found myself a big, heavy, stiff, slow-moving man moving almost painfully along a street. All the sights around me appeared familiar to one half of me, and entirely unfamiliar to the other half. I was awake, but how strangely awake. What a roar of harsh sounds, grinding wheels, clanging bells, discordant and angry voices, and what faces – stern, hard, selfish, smileless, sickly, pale, wrinkled, careworn, ugly as with sinful passion, and yet these are human faces and being human they are capable of happiness, though not one appears happy. And the buildings – how tall and dark, how massed together. I suppose this is what we used to have on our world in the ancient days, and that it is called a city. Clock tower, town hall, Collins Street, five o'clock; this information comes to the slow and heavy half of me. And yet this slow half is part of me, and its automatic movements carry me past tram and bus and through moving wheels, in and out, without danger. Down Swanston Street, with half of me knowing and half of me dreaming, I move through noise, smoke, dust; crushing and crowding to a station and a train, and cries of "hurry up! hurry up!" A slamming and a banging, a hoarse shriek, a jerk and we are moving to the accompaniment of grinding and roaring. Surely here the main study of everyone is how to make life miserable for everybody else.

'More clang and bang, more roar and shriek, more hurry and rush and crush, more striving to be first through narrow gates and then we are in a suburb. Here the buildings are farther apart, and there is a patch of garden ground here and there, but these are mostly neglected. Home? Yes, and that elderly lady my wife? Why she is older than my mother's mother. That bearded pard my son? He is surely older than my father. "Come along, Dad; you look a bit tired. Had a lot of stair climbing today I suppose."

~

"Yes, my son. It is as I thought; you are living a double life."

'I looked around, dazed. My old friend is sitting opposite, and a gentle oscillation now and then reminds me that I am in a railway train travelling one hundred miles an hour towards the metropolis of Mars. Four broad gauge lines: two central ones for express traffic and outside lines for stopping trains.

"I hope you will excuse me. I do not understand. Must have been asleep, sorry—"

"No! No, boy. I was just telling you; you are living a double life."

"Oh! I remember; you sent me into something like sleep, and I have had a strange dream."

"That was no dream; it was an episode. Just half-an-hour of the other life you are living. I was with you all the time, and I saw and heard all that you saw and heard. On Earth you are about sixty-three years of age. These years are about half the length of ours, you know. You are in business as a commission agent in Melbourne, the capital of Australia; you have a wife to whom you have been married thirty-eight years, and your eldest son, whom you saw, is about twice your age. He is nearly thirty-seven, and a family man."

"But I know nothing of this; how is it possible?"

"That I cannot explain. The phenomenon is rare, but it is mine as well as yours. I am an Earthborn, and forty years ago, Earth-years, I was teaching at a school in that very city of Melbourne, then an infant city. I transferred about that time, but have not lost my interest in Earth-life, and I keep a constant lookout for such as you. That is my reason for ascertaining your identity. Sooner or later I should have sought you had not accident thrown us together."

"You say 'transferred' about forty years ago?"

"Yes, that is what I call it. My soul, or the Ego, had no further use for its earthly tenement, and so transferred itself or was transferred by a Higher Power to its present one."

"Pardon my inquisitiveness. I feel that I am stepping on ground that must be sacred to you. Can you tell me anything about what we call death, seeing that you have evidently undergone it?"

"I can tell you but little. For some years I suffered from a painful cancer, and grew weaker and worse until I had to give up my occupation. I longed then for death, as it is termed, although I knew that I was living elsewhere. One hot day I sat weakly, gasping and longing for a cool breath, when I felt a strange fulness at the heart, a spasm of pain, and then a sweet sleep stole over me – a feeling of calm and perfect rest. I woke here feeling fuller of life than ever, and perfectly happy. You now know all that I do. Birth and death appear to me very much alike in some respects. One brings us from we know not whence into life and consciousness, and the other lets us lapse into unconsciousness, and we go we know not whither. Possibly life is a day and death a night, and the real life – the life of an immortal – is a succession of such changes taking place at longer or shorter intervals."

"And death as we usually know it; not the transference that you have undergone and that I may undergo – what think you of that?"

"I regard it as a natural change, and although I know nothing of its results, nothing of what will become of me when it again takes place, I do not fear it, for the Master of Life and Death is on both sides of the grave, and what He has appointed must be the best thing possible. But to return to the subject; I think we were speaking of life not death."

"Yes; I was about to ask you if your consciousness or lack of it was similar to my own."

"In some respects it was, but I was born younger than you. I commenced life on Mars when about thirty; you were evidently about forty-five. I had lived here ten Martial years before I became fully conscious. I had dim perceptions of some life outside, and some ideas came from the lower world, but I did not know of the dual life. Probably such knowledge would have been bad for me: imagine a baby, having even in the form of dreams, the experiences of a man. The baby would surely die; his brain would not endure the strain of double consciousness."

"Then I may become conscious of Earth-life at any time?"

"You may, and when you do so there will be a period of great mental confusion. I would like to have you near me then, for having gone through it I can help you to put the two classes of ideas in order."

"Do you think the Earth-dwelling half of me is conscious?"

"I know he is: he has kept a record of his actions in your body and may reveal them to his Earth-peers. I was conscious in the same way, at first thinking that I had strange dreams. I kept a sort of cursory record, but it has been lost long ago."

"Did you not say that you continue to take an interest in Earth-life?"

"I did say so, and I am sorry that you can give me so little direct information. I learned a good deal from you during the half hour of your trance; I saw the heart of Melbourne, and gleaned from that many sociological facts. Australia has advanced materially since I last learned anything. When you obtain consciousness, you will be able to tell me much that I would like to know regarding the Sunny South; at present, however, you have all to learn. The Earth side of you can draw a few comparisons; he can see that the two civilisations are widely different; but that is far the duller half. The Earth-body is opaque and heavy, and its brain responds but slowly to the stimulus of the soul. It is more an automaton than anything else. What thought you of the appearance of the people of Melbourne?"

"I thought them unhappy," I replied. "I but once saw a smiling face, and that appeared to smile as if selfishly gratified. There seemed to be a rich abundance of good things, and many pretty ones. The people, too, seemed to carry about with them a deal of personal property, as if they liked to show that they had it – a thing we never think of – and those who dwelt in the houses massed together in such ugly confusion appeared to have filled their windows with all they possessed. Behind one piece of glass I saw beautiful and strange flowers, but behind another there were heaped, shapeless lumps of animal matter. On the whole I did not like what I saw, and I wonder how my Earth-half endures it."

"Still, the civilisation you found in Melbourne is considered high, and its people are reckoned as very progressive."

"Then why such heat and dust? Why such foul smells? Why so much hurrying and crushing? And why, if they are a civilised people, are they all striving to be first, to get best places, as they did at the railway station? Our crowds are far bigger than theirs, but we never push each other about and speak harshly. We can dispose of our crowd in half the time they can, or less."

"I will answer some of these questions for you, my son, some other time; meanwhile I may tell you the reason for the general unhappiness – it is selfishness. All those people are trying to get and hold the good things of life for themselves and their families. They are not yet aware that happiness is found in seeking to benefit others."

"We are slowing down; is this the Ocean Terminus?"

"It is. We have now to go five thousand two hundred miles by sea. It is twenty hours since we met my son, and I seem to have known you as many years. If, without putting any passenger to inconvenience, we can spend our time on board together now and then I shall be grateful. The society of a young and intelligent man or woman is gratifying to me, especially if I see that the gratification is mutual. Do not, however, devote all your time to me; there will be hundreds of young people whom you do not know, and you may form profitable acquaintances. If by any chance we get separated, do me the favour of making my house the first place of call. The Central Executive has had the kindness to give me a residence exactly opposite the principal entrance to the Metropolitan Museum."

'Quietly and gently our great express comes to a stand, and we get out. We have no need to trouble about our luggage; it will be taken care of by the officials until we want it. No thieves will steal it; even in the great metropolis there are no prisons. The platform we step on is composed of springy rubber, and the footways in the streets of the port – Port Howard as it is called – are of the same material. It is pleasant to walk upon, and the feet make no sound.

'My elderly companion, whom I now know as having a worldwide fame as a mathematician, Andrew Grayson, takes the lead, and in a few minutes we find ourselves in a great hostel with some thousand guests. We find that a vessel leaves in an hour and another in two days, but that the former has to call at two southern ports while the latter goes direct. My companion decides for me; we will wait two days. There are some objects of interest he desires to show me.

'It is late in the afternoon. We had partaken of dinner in the train. There was still a couple of hours before dark, but not time for any extended excursion. My companion, whom I discovered to have a weakness – pardonable in a man of his age – for warmth and quiet, elected to rest in his cosy sitting room. I went out for a walk by the sea shore. It was my first view of the ocean. I had read of it and seen sea pictures in the work of some of the first artists of our planet, but I did not realise the vastness of the scene until brought face to face with it.

'Its ceaseless motions impressed me most strangely. It was never still; it appeared like an awful monster having a life of its own. Of course I knew that each time the moon passed over, it caused a small tide; and that the outer satellite passed over once in thirty hours, causing another; and that occasionally the ocean was acted upon by both at once. There are men of science who say that if we were deprived of our satellites, our two great oceans would stagnate and kill us all by their putridity.

'I spent hours by the sea shore, and saw how my journey had displaced the constellations. The Southern Cross and the Darkened Window were barely above the horizon, and the moons were both passing overhead. Then the little one suddenly dropped into the shadow of its primary. I went to my hostel and, full of new and strange thoughts, went to sleep.

∿

'Early next morning my friend Grayson asked me to accompany him to one of the sights of Port Howard. I was ready and willing, and in a few moments we were in a small air boat going towards a mountain that on one side bounded our horizon. In an hour we landed on the top of it.

"What think you of the view?" asked Grayson.

"It is far the vastest I have seen, and with the ocean and sky on one hand, and the great plain all around, it can be called grand. But it is beautiful also, for I do not see a space of neglected or uncultivated ground."

"Quite true. I brought you here to show you one of the greatest works ever attempted by man. For several thousands of years this was a desolate swamp; prior to that time it was a shallow sea, and earlier still a deep sea. To explain these changes I should have to go into the geological history of the planet, with which you are already conversant. For you have been taught that at one time we had more sea than land, and that water in actual quantity and in space occupied is gradually but surely diminishing."

"Yes. Gaston, our teacher, told us that in one of his delightful talks; he also said that the human and other dwellers on our planet at that time had more water in their composition."

"He was right. And what was true of our planet then is true of the Earth at present. The body in which you spent half-an-hour the other day is four-fifths water; the one in which you dwell today has a higher temperature, is less dense, is lighter and more active, and is not quite half water. Possibly nature means something by making changes of structure come about gradually with changes of surroundings. But we are here to study a work of man as helping nature. All the land that we see from this mountain top, and thousands of miles that we cannot see, lay for thousands of years a pestiferous swamp. Here and there was a deep lagoon, and here and there a patch of tropical forest. Reptiles, wading birds and deadly snakes were the principal inhabitants of this vast area. For hundreds of miles on all sides, the land was rendered unhealthy by this dreadful space that seemed not to know whether to be water or land. The wind that passed over this region carried miasma[10] and death with it upon all sides. People had to live in this miasmatic area, for the soil was rich and bread was wanted. Thousands of deaths occurred every year from atmospheric poisoning yet still the land was tilled, and in a while people were bred who seemed to thrive on poison."

---

10 The miasmatic theory of illness, which pre-dated and competed with germ
   theory, posited that illness stemmed from vapours known as 'miasmas' that
   emanated from unhealthy environments.

"That I should call a case of local adaptation. A moment ago you spoke of planetary adaptation of structure to surroundings."

"Just so. It is a question of time and degree: in one a modification of heredity renders a few families incapable of suffering certain complaints; in the other whole species and races of beings subdue themselves and their surroundings by adaptation of one to the other by gradual, and probably almost imperceptible, changes."

"And how was this great change finally brought about? How do we get a mountain and a rich and fertile plain where for ages there was such a waste?" asked I.

"We get it from the brain of a great engineer. A man planned the work and it took nearly two hundred years to accomplish. The reclaimed land is called the Central Plain, but the mountain on which we stand is called Mount Weston, after John Weston, who designed the whole work. The land is nearly one-twentieth of the land surface of the planet. Two beautiful rivers drain it, and the great trunk line on which we travelled yesterday runs right through it. It is, as you see, an agricultural land, and thinly populated. We do not put city areas upon built lands. Thinly populated as it is, however, no less than fifty branch lines from north and south are required for its produce and passengers. The lines are part of the plan. The engineer seemed to know what would be wanted from the beginning."

"From whence did he get all the material used?"

"He got all of it from the underground lines. Of these, a dozen were being pushed forward at once, and some of the material has travelled over four thousand miles. The first survey occupied Weston and a staff of one hundred men for five years. To begin with an air boat could not cross, because one could not carry electricity enough. Cables had to be laid and stations erected, and the course of the two rivers was partly determined by the lagoons; they were found in some places to form chains and flow into each other. They flow into the sea with currents a quarter of a mile wide and twenty feet deep, and they are navigable along their whole length, and are much used in the carriage of building material and heavy traffic.

"Weston worked on a definite plan. In draining and filling, he took care not to bury any soil or material that could enrich the soil. As he brought up the level of the dry land he covered it with soil and made it into farms, and built houses on piles. In many places he put sleeping rooms in the air on piles twenty feet high, for he found that by getting so far above ground that many people ceased to suffer from malarial complaints.

"As a result of his wise action, his army of workers soon grew food enough to sustain them, and as they pushed ever forward with their enterprise they left rich and cultivated land behind them. This was rapidly disposed of and rendered ever more and more fertile by good management."

"And the mountain; it also must have been built?"

"True. When the plain was well-nigh finished, the engineers found that they would have some millions of yards of material to spare. They decided to pile it in one vast heap and to plant the heap with forest trees, and make it into an elevated reserve and a monument of the engineer for ever. The plough has never to touch its surface, and the small and harmless animals and birds that congregate here have never to be hunted unless they become too numerous and damage the crops on the plain. As for the evil beasts that dwelt in the swamp, they are all exterminated."

"That is the case all over the planet, is it not?"

"I am thankful to say that it is: more than that, many noxious and poisonous insects have been abolished by our improvements, and even dangerous animalculæ have gone the same way. We found out that our most dangerous foes could only be seen under the microscope many ages ago, and we fought them. They were more dangerous and more to be dreaded than tigers or lions, wolves or snakes. In the foolish war times, they were more deadly than the sword."

"You have certainly shown me a great wonder, and have made it into one of the best object lessons I have ever had. How I wish that you could spare the time to show me some more of our wonderful world."

"A wonderful world indeed, and principally made such since the Federation of the Nations and the Declaration of Eternal Peace. Naturally, ours is but a little third-rate planet, a ragged starveling, cold by reason of its distance from the sun. When all our armies and navies were disbanded, the labour market was swamped and the Grand Federal Government had to consider the problems of labour and bread. It was then that army contingents were sent to the waste places to purify them and make them fertile, and the men worked together and had a common speech, and married and settled on the reclaimed lands, and in time forgot their national prejudices and became one nation. Had we not united in some such way, these great works could not have been undertaken, and our little planet would only have maintained in comfort about one-tenth of its present number of inhabitants. But we must go and dine, and then I will show you a case of perpetual motion."

"Where shall we dine? We are one hundred miles or so from our hostel."

"Steer for the nearest house in the direction of yonder point, for we will visit that after dinner."

'By steering north five miles and east three, we came to a caravansary near the foot of the mountain, and were well supplied with all we could desire. After dinner my companion desired to rest an hour, and I was left to my own reflections. I went and took a seat in a small arbour that opened upon a pretty lawn and small flower garden, beyond which was a rich vegetable garden surrounded by fruit trees. Further into the open plain, men at work were preparing the ground for the first crop.

"Ahem! Ahem!" says a voice behind me. I looked round and saw an elderly woman almost behind me. I moved aside, apologised for not having seen her and for my intrusion, and offered to withdraw.

"Nay, my young friend, it was not for that reason that I made my presence known. I saw you at dinner in company with the world-known Grayson and wished then to know more of you, and especially to learn how you came to possess the Badge of Freedom at such an early age."

'I gave her an account of my father's work and mine.'

CHAPTER XI

Mars and Malthus

'**M**Y RECITAL AROUSED the elderly lady, and evidently called to mind some familiar chains of thought. Said she:

"Are you aware that your discovery has once more answered an old chain of fallacious reasoning?"

"No, I know nothing of any reasoning that I have answered."

"Then I will tell you of something fresh to your mind. I am Edith Somers. Some people call me Doctor Somers, and I have written a little on social science. I have said that our world is not yet fully populated; that discoveries may any day be made that will double our resources. Such a discovery you have made. By its use, the snow line, north and south, will be driven back, and millions of acres of useless land made available for tillage and the residence of happy men and women. And by its use, this very land upon which we are looking will probably have its productiveness doubled."

"You are much more sanguine than I am regarding the ultimate effects of my experiments. It is nevertheless my intention to try the snow lines. Good may be done there. As for tropical plains such as this, I do not think their productiveness can be much increased. And further, we have yet to see whether or not land will be impoverished by being made to produce more rapidly and freely. We have already come to the conclusion that chemical elements have to be supplied in greater quantities, though so far our experiments have left us in a little doubt. Certainly I do not expect to be responsible for any vast increase in our population."

"Still my idea is that you have done more for us than Weston did when he drained our great swamp and gave to the world this fair land. You have provided an answer for the Croakers, and I have great hopes for the future of your discovery, especially seeing you so young and full of life, and evidently bent on making the most of a great thing."

"Who are the Croakers you speak of?"

"They are writers who from time immemorial, from the very depths of almost prehistoric periods, have complained of the population being too numerous. They have always found that population increased more rapidly than the means of subsistence, and have threatened us with universal famine in a few years or, at most, a few generations."

'Grayson, joining us after his hour of rest, said, "Yes, my son. What Doctor Somers tells you is quite true, and it may astonish you to learn that what is true of Mars is equally true of the Earth. It, according to the disciples of a well-meaning man named Malthus,[11] is in danger of overpopulation."

11 Political economist and clergyman Thomas Robert Malthus (1766–1834) refuted the utopian visions of English philosopher William Godwin (1756–1836) and French polymath Nicolas de Condorcet (1743–1794), who claimed that, as humanity followed an inevitable trajectory of improving morality and knowledge, each population would naturally arrive at a balance of maximised human contentment that did not strain the limits of the

"But that cannot be, the Earth is a large planet and very young. It is seven times the bulk of ours, and is lighter, warmer and more moist. I have read that it is thinly populated, that only about twelve-hundred-million human dwellers inhabit it; that its productions are mostly consumed by animals, and that there are millions of square miles that have never been trodden by human feet. Until the other day I read these statements with some doubt, but now I only wonder that the history and literature of the Earth are not incorporated with those of Mars."

"To some extent they are," said Doctor Somers. "My old friend Andrew Grayson and I are both acquainted with the main outlines of the history of the Earth, and we have read some of the productions of Homer and Shakespeare."

"Excuse my negligence, Doctor Somers," said Grayson. "I ought to have introduced Charles Frankston to you at dinner time, and to have told you that he is an Earthborn and yet incorporated there, though not hitherto conscious on this side of his being. That was my reason for mentioning Malthus when I so unceremoniously joined in your conversation."

"Say nothing about that, my valued friend. Have not we been acquainted for ten years or more?" said the physician. "I was telling Frankston that his discovery had provided an answer to the population of Croakers who from age to age threaten us with starvation and advise us to

<hr>

planet's bounty. One *Melbourne and Mars* reviewer noted the prominence in the book of 'castigation of the followers of Malthus' (*Weekly Times*, Melbourne, 7 December 1889, 7). See also: Thomas Malthus, *An Essay on the Principle of Population* (London: J Johnson, 1798); William Godwin, *An Enquiry Concerning Political Justice, and its Influence on General Virtue and Happiness*, 4th ed, 1842; Paul Warde, Libby Robin and Sverker Sörlin, *The Environment: A History of the Idea* (Baltimore: Johns Hopkins University Press, 2018), 58–59.

cease marrying, or to marry when life has lost the charm of youth."

"So it has, though I have not yet mentioned that side of the matter to him. Each human being who is brought into the world brings a mouth to feed, but also two hands with which to feed it. Given a sphere of labour, each worker will provide more than he consumes. One man working there in the open can grow more provision than one hundred can eat; but that one man, as a troglodyte in his cave, might find life hard if he had to gather shellfish and catch swimming ones for a family of four."

"The world must have been over populated many times," said I, "for it has undergone so many changes. We keep no large animals now, but each cow must have eaten the food of ten humans?"

"The cow", said Doctor Somers, "was quite a tolerable being; not nearly so wasteful as some; its milk, butter and cheese were handy though highly concentrated articles of food, and we killed it and ate its flesh. Every portion of it was useful. The hog was more wasteful: it only gave its dead carcase; returning probably one hundredth part of what it had devoured."

"It was frequently diseased, was it not?" I asked.

"Yes! It was a strumous[12] beast and people who consumed much of its flesh grew coarse. It carried many kinds of parasites into humans and actually lowered the moral tone, making people more sensual. It was a red-letter day in our calendar when we decided that it should breed no more."

---

12 'Strumous', from 'struma', relating to the infection and swelling of the lymph nodes often associated with tuberculosis. Also known as 'scrofula'.

"The animal whose extinction I most regret", remarked Grayson, "was the horse."

"But he is not extinct," answered Doctor Somers. "There are hundreds yet in use in the stone quarries of Kempton and in the marble quarries of Middleham."

"True! But he is doomed; it takes all that an acre of rich land can grow to feed him; he cannot compete with electricity that eats nothing, and he is not so hardy as the ass who picks up his food by the wayside, and does not leave his home. Our feathered friends and a few small playfellows will be all our animals in a few years hence."

"Very probably," said Doctor Somers; "but after all, a human life is more valuable than an animal one, and being capable of more happiness, ought to be encouraged."

"So it is," assented Grayson. "And more than that, humans themselves are always undergoing selection; nature at the last only conserves the best. The criminal, the pauper, the vagrant, the selfish livers have in turn all had to go. Even the few mostly harmless lunatics found in our asylums are fewer in number each decade, and the number of incurables in our hospitals does not increase. The rigour of our long winters used to kill thousands of our people, but now pulmonary diseases are very rare. Today we are more numerous, longer lived, healthier and more prosperous, happier than we have ever been."

"What is the number of our population?" I asked.

"In round numbers, five thousand two hundred and thirty-seven million – about four times the present population of the Earth. We are not at a standstill; there is a gradual increase still going on. We number four times as many as dwell on the Earth, and that planet is far larger and its resources greater. When the Earth has twenty thousand millions of people upon its surface, it will not be densely populated," answered Grayson.

"The Malthusian idea need not trouble Earth-dwellers for some ages," I remarked, looking at Doctor Somers, whom I could see had something to say.

'The doctor drew her seat forward and came to where the light revealed her more fully. I then saw that she was a grand and handsome woman, with clearly defined features, a massive forehead, and eyes that seemed capable of at once revealing her soul and exploring the innermost recesses of those around her. She was not young; she might be five and twenty, but her face was unwrinkled, and her hair a wavy brown without a thread of gray in it.

'I learned afterwards that she was a distinguished physician and a metropolitan teacher of physiology.

'Slowly and impressively the doctor began to speak. Evidently she meant to say something final regarding Malthusianism, as taught in both worlds. She said: "We have been speaking in a cursory manner about a subject to which I have paid much thoughtful attention, and about which I feel deeply. These worlds are the creations of the Divinity; the father and mother God rules beneficently in both. We may take it for granted that He knows something about mating and governing planets of various sizes and kinds, and adapting life to its surroundings. Here are two populations, both human, both civilised to a certain extent, both morally responsible, both religious in pro-portion to capacity, and yet both doubting and fearing. Why is this? Our Maker has fitted us in all respects to our surroundings. Put an Earth-man on Mars, and the internal pressure of air would explode him, and if he could endure our comparatively rarefied air, he would not be able to adapt his muscles to our half-pressure gravitation. With our light he could hardly see, and even our summer temperature would starve him. Our temperate zones in winter would remind him of Greenland and Spitzbergen; our frosts would certainly congeal his great watery body. Put a Martial-man on Earth and the density of the atmosphere would crush his organs together; his muscles would not enable him to drag along; the moist, hot air would suffocate him; the light would blind him, and though a man on Mars, he would appear a dwarf amongst the larger and more burly, muscular Earth-men. Surely if the Deity has made humans with so much in common and yet so different, he has in other respects adapted them to the worlds they occupy.

"The human race grows upon its planet as an individual grows. It is at first little, weak and inefficient; then it gains strength and grows more rapidly. In a while it attains to its full size, but is not educated, matured, perfected. As it lives on it improves, becomes more sensible, more intelligent, more moral; it purges itself of selfishness and becomes more altruistic. A race life is the same. The race on Earth is young yet; it is that of a child. It has not yet learned to talk properly; its nations remind us of children heaping up ridges of sand and saying 'This is my house', and fighting if one knocks down a wall and claims two shares. So far the race has wasted most of its force in fighting for small slices of cultivated land, while three-fourths of the Earth is yet a wilderness. Arbitration between nations is but commencing, and Federation of a few of the most civilised and powerful nations is but a dream of the future. They are where we were a thousand years before the Declaration of Eternal Peace, and our population has increased fivefold since then. It may yet increase, may even double again and be easily sustained.

"Science has told us this; nothing is more sensitive than population. If there is room for expansion it expands, if life becomes harder it remains stationary, and if the conditions become painfully severe, as in the Black Century, it decreases, and all this without any special action of optimist or pessimist. When a planet is full of happy human life the race may be said to have attained to manhood and maturity. It may then remain full until the conditions again change, and the human life and that of the planet pass into senility together. If there are any creators then their cry will be that the race is growing old and ceasing to be productive.

"Whatever does put a check upon population, be sure that it will not be a painful thing: war, famine, pestilence and the like are said to be the natural checks, but these cannot be. For long before the race can attain full growth, altruism must abolish war, cleanliness must make pestilence impossible, and as to famine – well, we have made provision already for several bad harvests of a worldwide extension. The check to the population of a planet is like the check to an individual. On Earth, men grow and reach six feet in height; on Mars they reach but four feet, and yet one is not conscious of his bigness nor the other of his littleness, for each is adapted to his surroundings and circumstances, and what is true of the atom, is true of the whole."

'The doctor paused and seemed for a moment afraid that her zeal had carried her too far. I set her mind at rest on that score by saying, "Thank you, Doctor, for your lucid reasoning of the question; your verbal answer to the Croakers is surely superior to the practical one that you kindly placed to my credit. They have not a leg left to stand on. How I wish that your argument could be conveyed to the Malthusians of Earth, for there surely the idea of over population is absurd."

"What Doctor Somers says will be written on Earth in a few hours," said Grayson. "You will write it there. All you have to do is to see that your diary does not get lost like mine was."

"Indeed," said the doctor. "Frankston is a diarist then?"

"He is, though strange to say he does not know it on this side of his being. If he should become conscious on both sides he will convey a vast amount of information to both worlds. I hope to introduce him to the club of the Earthborn when we get to the metropolis."

"I, too, shall be pleased to meet him; not at that club, for I have no right to enter that I know of, but in my own home."

"Be sure that I shall make the most of your invitation," I answered.

'We separated, to spend the latter part of the afternoon each in our own way, Grayson remarking that we would remain the night here and spend the morning in visiting the sights he promised me. He made arrangements for our catching the boat at Port Howard at sixteen in the afternoon of next day. I climbed Mount Weston on foot, and had a final view of the plain at sunset.

~

'The next morning found Grayson and myself at an early hour flying rapidly towards a distant point on the plain. It was soon reached, and we entered a small building at the source of one of the rivers previously mentioned. We went down a spiral staircase and entered a little room, one side of which had a wall moving in a circular movement in a close-fitting bed of what appeared to be bronze.

"What is this?" I asked.

"It is the axle of one of Weston's great wheels," answered Grayson. "It has never ceased to revolve for two hundred years."

"Strange that it has not worn out in that time."

"Had these been common steel and common bronze they would have been, but these metals are so tempered that a diamond will not cut them. There are three of these wheels here, and several more at low places on the plain. They are each one hundred feet in diameter and twelve feet wide. They scoop up the water and pour it into the aqueduct."

'We went through another door into a larger room that contained a model of the three wheels. It was set in motion by a small electric motor – a reduced model of the one that drives the wheels. The model one needs but a thread to drive it; the great one has its power carried by a thick cable. From one end of the model room we can look down into the cistern that catches the water from a score of great drains, and we can see the ascending buckets so slung that the movement of the great wheel does not spill the water back again until the proper place for tilting is reached. Were it not for these wheels, much of the great plain would again become swampy. The water thrown up by these wheels is sufficient to make a respectable river to begin with. About a mile downstream the water flows very slowly, and the river is deep and clear. From this point it is used as a waterway for the carriage of produce, manures and similar. Railway lines run under the rivers at many points.

"This great work is one that no syndicate or company could have undertaken. It is one that would heavily tax the resources of a great nation. Such works are only possible to a peaceful federation of nations," said Grayson, as we came away, "and on your planet, there are several such works waiting for the time when international action is possible. For instance, which nation will attempt to make Sahara into a sea, while its possession might have to be fought for by several European powers?"

'Two hours later we were dining at Port Howard, and in another hour our great boat, with some two thousand passengers on board, was swiftly moving across the central ocean.'

CHAPTER XII

More Wonders

'W E WHO DWELL on Mars, a planet that has lost its water surface to some extent and increased its land in like proportion, do not travel much by sea. Millions never see the oceans, even though they travel at times a good deal. Still, in so vast a population of happy and healthful people living under a benign and well-nigh perfect legislation, there are many who travel for information and pleasure, and many whose occupation necessitates constant movement. Some spend the greater part of their forty-nine days in travel, and some go to a warmer zone for the winter in order to work there.

'The travelling accommodation of the planet is sometimes severely taxed. So much so that the Central Executive advise certain trades to take their holidays at certain periods or between certain months at their convenience, so that too many may not be on the move at one time.

'This ocean boat, though not one of the largest, can berth and accommodate two thousand five hundred people. It has three decks available for passengers extending from end to end of the ship. The work of the ship is done on the fourth deck. The great motors work there, and the accumulators – weighing some three thousand tons – are stored in the lowest hold as ballast.

'Long voyages have not to be provided for; there is not room in our oceans for a long voyage. We travel nearly one hundred miles an hour, and so complete our ocean journey in little more than two days. Our boat looks very plain; there are no masts, spars nor funnels. Nothing on the upper deck but the bridge, the cook's kitchens and the ventilators for the lower decks.

'Providing for us all is a very easy task; as on land we have but one meal, except the little breakfast for mothers and young children, and this meal, though good and plentiful, very rarely consists of more than two courses. We have very little waste of food. Plates are not sent away with their contents almost untasted, because other courses on the card are likely to be more palatable.

'During our brief voyage, I made the acquaintance of several young men and women who were going to the metropolis for the purpose of passing examinations or for study. They were all remarkably eager and intelligent, but our conversations were none of them exactly worthy of being recorded.

'At twenty-one o'clock of the third day, after a run of fifty-five hours over smooth waters, we drew near the port of Granby – the greatest western port of the central ocean. I went to the cabin and called Grayson, as I had no desire to be separated from him. We saw a number of great boats. I had no idea that there were so many; going past them all was quite a long walk. About half of them were evidently used like the one we had just left, for passenger traffic only. There were also some very large cargo boats.

The concourse of people was very great. Many had come to welcome friends and relatives, and others were there for amusement. It was two hours after sunset, but the abundance of electric lights, none of which were permitted to glare or cast strong shadows, shed a soft radiance upon the scene and almost compensated for the absence of the sun.

'In spite of the crowd we were soon comfortably settled in our hostel. There are many large ones in Granby, this being the largest of a ring of ports surrounding the central ocean. Here we had the same springy, silent paths and freedom from dust, noise and dirt that I noticed in Port Howard. As in all other places, the houses were not crowded together; there is no need for anything of the kind. Most of the workers prefer to travel a few miles when the labours of the day are over. The great depots are built close together and as near to the loading wharves as possible, but there is no visible traffic between them and the ships. Yet, a boat containing many thousands of tons is unloaded or loaded in a day of five hours, the load passing along tubes; some pneumatic, some containing small railways, and some an Archimedean screw.

'Grayson and I did not spend any time amongst these wonders, as they were to my provincial eyes, though he advised me to see some of them when opportunity served, as a mechanic could not know too much about machinery.

'Next morning I was up with the sun and got a good view of Granby – the wharves and piers and the ocean – from a tower built on an eminence in one of the ornamental recreation grounds in the city. From the top of Mount Weston I had seen the sun sink apparently into a bed of liquid fire, and from my present stand I saw him rise as if from the same bed.

'His coming was heralded by the tuneful voices of thousands of feathered songsters, who lifted up their songs of praise; and I hope I may be pardoned for saying that I felt so full of happiness and life, so thankful for all the good things placed in my pathway that I, too, out of pure joy and gladness, sang a prayer of thanksgiving.

"Amen," said a deep, strong voice behind me. I turned quickly and looked into the eyes of a man. Large and dark were these eyes, and full of depth and power. He was a strong and sturdy man in the very prime of early manhood, being apparently about seventeen years of age. His head, face, attitude and general appearance all told of physical and mental strength and force of character.

"Yes, Amen," he repeated. "Nothing gives me greater pleasure than to see the happiness of youth, and to hear it ascribed to the proper source, the Giver of Good."

"Can we ascribe good to any other source?" I asked.

"Not directly, but some people are ungrateful, some proud, some indifferent. We are not yet perfect in this best of possible worlds. However, I have a purpose in interrupting your Matin[13] song: you are Charles Frankston; your friend Grayson sent for me an hour ago, and finding you had gone out he asked me to follow you, adding that you would be sure to go to the nearest eminence."

"My old friend must be very observant. I have only travelled with him five days, and in that time have only climbed Mount Weston."

"Probably he has read the aspiring, climbing, up-striving nature in your features."

'By this time we were nearly back at the hostel, but instead of going in we met Grayson, who introduced the

13 In the Christian tradition, a 'Matin' is an early morning service of devotion.

stranger as Harry Brand, the Electrical Engineer-in-Chief for the Port of Granby. Hearing of the important position he held, I was no longer surprised that he should be a man of power of body and mind; an average man could not control interests so vast. He and his staff had to keep in working order the thousands of miles of transmitters that supply heat, light and power to houses and manufactories, and also to provide the motive power used in the scores of great depots mentioned. In addition to this, they had to be ready to charge three or four thousands of tons of accumulators in the holds of the great ships.

"Our friend Brand", said Grayson, taking my arm as we walked along, "is going to take us down into a hole some seven miles deep, and show us where he gets his electricity from."

"Have you been before?" asked I.

"No," replied Grayson. "I have frequently promised my-self the pleasure, but have found some reason hitherto for hurrying past. This time I have two strong young men to help me, and I am not tied for time."

'As he spoke, we drew near one of the red balls mounted on the top of a post, indicating to travellers by air boat where they can drop to charge with electricity. Close to it was a little building placed over a stairway that appeared to lead straight down towards the centre of the planet. We all three went down the stairs, Brand taking the lead.

'The stairway was a spiral one of fifty steps, and at the bottom we found an open space, a few small rooms and a combination of closed car with electric motor, this being adapted for the carriage of four people, one of whom had to manipulate the machinery. Grayson and I were going straight to the car, which was obviously intended for our use, when Brand called us back.

"It will be necessary", says he, "for you, my friends, to remove your outer clothing and put on these garments. And when we have to leave the car, these will have to be added," pointing to helmets with clear glass fronts and little knapsacks at the back. "Were you to attempt the journey as you are, you would never return."

'In a few minutes we had made the exchange and taken our seats, and the car began to move rapidly down an incline.

"This car", remarked Brand, "is made of glass, and the outer clothing you are now wearing is also glass. We shall probably have to pass through what will appear very dangerous, and we shall not be able to speak to each other; in such cases follow me."

"I was not aware", said Grayson, "that we were taking such risks in visiting your domain. It is scarcely fair to young Frankston, for an old man like me the risk is less. I am at the end of my usefulness; he is just beginning his."

"It is true", said Brand, "that our risks increase, but we have made such an important find in the very bottom of our mine that in spite of risk, we cannot leave off increasing the danger. We have only forty men at work, and each man thoroughly understands the situation. All the men work under diver's conditions, lest a breath of air should carry a light flash through a man, and each tool is handled with thick insulators. Were a man to wear an insulator through, and touch a tool with his bare hand, he would be killed; but every man knows that. We are working with five changes of men, and not stopping night nor day, except for Sabbath. Indeed, I have an emergency permit from the Executive to work Sabbath also, if circumstances make that step necessary."

'All this time we were running down a pretty steep incline; about one in ten I estimated it. I could see that Brand was not using the motor, that he was only holding us back with a footbrake.

"How far have we to go," I asked.

"About seventy miles in this carriage, and then straight down another half mile."

"And this slope is about one in ten, is it not?"

"It is."

"Then we shall be seven miles below the surface when the car stops and another half mile. You go a great depth for your electricity at Granby," said I.

"We get something more than electricity here," replied Brand. "You will see shortly. We are more than half way, and I saw the storm signals at the electrometer as we passed. Whatever happens sit still, and have no fear."

'Blash! blash!! blash!!! Blue, red and blinding white light, accompanied by a crackling as of ten thousand little explosions, and then all was dark again. Was I struck blind? If so, the operation was painless, and I was not hurt in any other way. No, I could see again, and there was Brand at the brake, and the car was just going on as before, lit by its own lamp and sending rays before it by the headlight.

"That was a rather astonishing experience, Harry," said Grayson; "are we likely to have much more of it?"

"Yes, we shall see a lot of that kind. It is comparatively harmless. We might have walked through that and lived," said Brand. "We sometimes have to go through miles of what we call spearheads and flames, and to work amongst lightnings and thunders. So long as we are covered and insulated, we are quite safe; but the men who work here are classed as first rank, which is equal to double the pay of ordinary miners, for they have to have rare fortitude and courage."

'Again blaze and glare, this time in yellow light, while the cavern rumbled and roared with crashing, deafening, rock-pounding thunders. Bayonet-shaped streaks of white lightning, all the time shooting towards us and passing the car. Steadily on we went, Brand never showing a sign of tremor, and the car going no slower nor quicker, but just straight on and down and down.

'Darkness and silence again for about ten minutes, and then Brand says, "We are at our journey's end for the present, but before leaving the car we must put on our headpieces; without them we should not live a thousandth part of a second in such a storm as that we have just passed through. You have no need to be afraid as regards breathing; there is six hours store of air in that little knapsack."

'In a few moments we could only look at each other through a glass; we could not hear nor speak.

'Brand touched me on the shoulder and gave Grayson some sign, and we looked round and saw that a cage had come from somewhere out of the deep, and we were invited to enter.

'Down again and still down. I began to wonder if ever I should get to the surface and breathe the free air and see the sun again.

'The cage stopped and Brand got out and signed for us to follow. This we did, going erect and walking on a firm path. All the drives in the Martial mines are made secure, are well lit, and high enough and wide enough to permit free movement. We followed Brand for about a mile, and as we went we kept meeting little trucks running along a narrow railway. I could see that most of these trucks were laden with some kind of metal, but I did not try to find out what it was at that juncture.

'When we had walked about a mile, we turned down a side drive and went about two hundred yards further, and there we found several men cutting pieces out of a vast solid mass of bright, yellow metal. The mass was all round them. They seemed to be in a chamber with metal walls, and to be just chopping away at the walls to make the room larger. I could then see that they were getting out such a solid mass of copper as has never been seen nor heard in any of our mining annals before. Brand gave us each a piece, but could not say a word about it; and while we stood there, several flashes of fire appeared to come out of the wall. Though men were working at the face, they did not even turn away; the insulation of their bodies and tools being perfect, there was nothing to fear. Sometimes, however, the mine is filled as with a mass of flame; there is then danger from heat.

'Having shown us the working, and given us some idea of the vastness of the mass of pure copper to be cut out, Brand led us back to the bottom of the shaft. He rang for a cage and sent word that men were coming up. This appeared to be customary, the cage giving an overhead protection.

'Swiftly up we went, and I was not sorry to rise out of those stifling and dangerous depths. Suddenly, and with a jerk that threw us up to the roof of the cage, we stopped, and in a few seconds something heavy fell down upon the cage.

"What has happened?" I tried to say, but found that the mask and headpiece prevented utterance most effectively. Brand broke a corner off our roof and enabled us to look up. We could see coils of a broken rope, and up towards the mouth of the shaft a mass of what appeared to be fire. We were imprisoned in the shaft and could neither get up nor down. Brand wrote on a board for us the words, "An unusual electric storm is raging above us; imprisoned here until men can get through to help us; we have each four hours of air; cannot remove masks; a few breaths of what is around us would produce asphyxia and probably kill us; we must wait."

'For three hours we waited, and all the time the fires filled the shaft above us. Grayson was silent and almost motionless; Brand never ceased to watch for the coming of help; I grew anxious and frightened. I had no wish to die just on the threshold of what might be a grand and happy life.

'More time passed, and then we heard someone on the roof. We looked out. A man was trying to find the end of rope, evidently with the intention of drawing it up, splicing it and pulling up the cage. Brand put his watch up through the hole he had made and pointed out the time; he then wrote some instructions on a slip of paper. These the man took, and troubling no further about the cage, put himself in a sling of rope and got drawn rapidly upwards. His life and ours hung on that rope. If it got burnt with another storm he would fall, and Brand's instructions would never reach the surface. I learned afterwards that all the ropes used were insulated with glass fibre, the kind used in weaving the garments we wore. Brand tore away at the roof, and I helped him to make the hole larger. We made it so that one of us could have crept out, but we could do nothing with the heavy tangled coils of rope above us.

'More time passed and my head began to feel full and hot, and strange lights began to dance before my eyes. I then began to feel sleepy and dizzy, and a sickly, faint sensation stole over me. I made efforts to rally, and looked through Brand's glass at his face; it was very pale and troubled. He tore a piece of paper and wrote, "Do not breathe when they change h—", and then he staggered and would have fallen if I had not caught him. In a few seconds more we were both on the floor of the cage somehow, and the last thing I saw was something coming through the broken roof and Grayson taking hold of it.

'A little later – how much later I could not tell – I found Brand and Grayson leaning over me, and making the movements necessary to produce respiration. I rose to my feet; we all three shook hands. The fresh helmets Brand had sent for had come in time. We had each six hours more air – our lives were saved.

'Why had Grayson been so still? While we fumed about and looked up and worked, he sat still; why this indifference? He was a philosopher and a mathematician, and also an old man. He knew that he could make his air last longer by keeping still and breathing little, and so he was able to help us when no other help could get near. When Brand and I fell unconscious, he was ready to receive the headpieces that had come a few minutes too late, and with a skill and strength wonderful in a man of his years, he had half raised Brand and screwed off his helmet and put another on. Brand immediately recovered, and then the two did a like service for me; but I had been out of life for five minutes and did not rally so easily. Grayson had saved us all by his foresight and promptness.

'We could not yet speak, but we knew the danger was past, for the rope was going up from the roof and we should be drawn up long before our air was exhausted. In another hour we were being welcomed to the surface by some forty-two masked and insulated men. Of necessity there was no cheering, but the faces behind the glasses were cheerful and smiling, and the clasp of friendly hands was better than the embrace of death.

'The men below were now ringing for a cage. The shift had not come to relieve them at the usual time and so they had come to see what was the matter. They had to be hurriedly got up, I thought, but I learned afterwards that they could get fresh charges of air in their knapsacks at certain places in the mine, and had done so on this occasion; being in the shaft we had no such chance.

'Brand left the men to get up and down as best they could, and took Grayson and me to see the Granby cables. There were ten of them, each about eighteen inches in diameter, and apparently growing out of the solid rock. Each cable had in it a thousand insulated copper wires of various diameters, and a central core an inch through, meant to carry electricity to fill up the accumulators of ocean-going boats.

'Brand asked us if we were willing to go and see the loadstone quarries. They were within half a mile, and were not down a shaft. Grayson declined, but would wait in the insulated car till we came back. I, feeling sure that Grayson was weary enough and having had enough adventure for one day, declined also. We entered the car, removed our helmets, and in little more than an hour, and without further adventure, reached the surface.

'How strange the open air felt, and how old the day was; it was hard to believe that it wanted yet two hours of sunset, and that we had only been below eight hours. It seemed to me eight years since I had helped the birds to welcome the sun still shining.

'To the hostel we all three directed our steps, and over a late dinner recounted our feelings and sensations as we underwent them in enforced silence. Brand had the most to say, for he had to explain what we had seen.

"The find of copper you have seen", said he, "is one of the most fortunate of discoveries. The copper mines near the surface were almost worked out, and the demand for copper is very great, and will be for a long time to come. I had been trying to carry electricity through other media, but found it not so good as the copper."

"But this", said I, "is a very rich, heavy copper."

"Yes, I know what you are going to say," returned Brand; "it contains gold and silver. If there was a good market for gold it would pay to extract it; but you see jewellery is not much worn, personal possessions conferring no distinction, and the coinage days are past and gone. Your medal is issued by the Central, but so few of those are in use that a ton of gold might serve the Government indefinitely."

"And the shaft, is not that a very ancient means of getting down for metals?" asked Grayson. "I remember that the Earth-men used that means and similar winding gear, except for the motive power and the insulated rope."

"The shaft", answered Brand, "is an expedient. It is sunk where it is in order that it may not interfere with the railway extension. Next year the cars will go direct from the surface and the copper will be cut out in bricks. The spiral line will corkscrew itself five miles more downward, and the copper field will be uncovered."

"A spiral line," said I, very much astonished; "is the line we travelled today a spiral?"

"It is; and much of it is cut through solid loadstone, the kind of rock most used in accumulators. We get electricity, loadstone and copper from under our feet; part of the copper is under the ocean."

"And what has been done with all the material taken out of that immense spiral?" I enquired.

'Grayson answered: "Some of the hills in this district are like Mount Weston – artificial; they have been made hundreds of years ago. Granby is a very ancient port, and its electrical works date from the Black Century. Our friend Harry Brand has had a thousand predecessors, who have in turn made improvements, and carried out the original plan to its present stage of completion."

"And the copper?" I asked.

"That is a very fortunate find," said Brand, again taking the conversation; "we were boring to see how far the loadstone extended and cut into that bed. It lies as if a cavern had been run full of molten copper at some warm period, or as if a lake – of very uneven depths – had been filled and covered to its present depth during geological times."

"Today is not a fair sample of the days down there, I hope?" asked Grayson, looking very serious.

"No; I have not seen a storm rage so long for years as the one that kept us in that shaft. Nor have I had so narrow an escape since I have been connected with it; the rescuers made the mistake of acting as if we had recharged. When we left we had air for three and a half hours, and never expected any delay. Two minutes more would have finished us. The men below had no idea that anything had happened. The mine will be almost absolutely safe when we get down to it the proper way; meanwhile we shall soon have copper enough, and can give up the present working."

'Harry Brand shortly afterwards took his departure.'

CHAPTER XIII

To the Metropolis – Sidonia

'FOR TWO DAYS our train ran along the main line, stopping only to recharge the accumulators. This takes but a few minutes, and occurs at about the end of each five hundred miles. Grayson and I had many interesting conversations, and I profited not a little by association with a man who knew so much and had so ripe a mind. It appeared as if we could touch upon no topic with which he was not thoroughly acquainted. Though we were travelling underground he could tell me all about the surface above each part. He described it as being generally unequal and cavernous. He said that small plantations were placed on the summits for the purpose of growing wood, and that the slopes were mostly used for fruit growing. Reservoirs occupied all the spaces that could be conveniently dammed, and the plains and valleys were irrigated wherever water could be applied with advantage. Altogether he showed plainly enough that without labour and constant attention the land on this side of the ocean would be about as useless as that on the other side before Weston's scheme was worked out. I more and more admire my fellow humans when I see how rich and productive they have made a little third-rate and cold planet by their labour alone.

"'Metropolitan Central". As our train slowed down I saw these two words in large letters on a distant wall, not painted or gilded, but written in light. We had travelled a week and come nearly halfway round the planet. Grayson did not want to part with me, and I felt that I had found a second father, so we went together to his house. He promised to introduce me to the Earthborn's Club after dinner, when many of the members would have finished work for the day and would be found there. I had no hesitation in accepting Grayson's hospitality, for he, having the freedom of the planet, cannot be put to any expense.

'Having performed my ablutions and made a few changes, my first action was a walk through a small part of the museum. I say a small part, for it will take weeks to visit all of it. The first thing to which I gave serious attention was a map of the metropolis. As I have to complete my studies here, and probably make this my home for many years, I wish to know all I can about it. It is a most magnificent capital. It is rectangular in shape, and the equator crosses its centre. From the equator it extends five hundred miles north and south, and its width is five hundred miles.

'The Grand Avenue follows the equator for five hundred miles, and is crossed at exactly its centre by the Central Avenue, which runs a thousand miles in a straight line north and south; each of these avenues is a quarter of a mile wide. At night these, and in fact all the streets, are lit by the electric light. Having seen the supply for Granby I began to wonder what would be required for this city.

'I remembered reading somewhere about our next neighbour's astronomers having found a long, straight line on Mars, something that indicated human handiwork. Can they have seen our city lit up? Or was the line our avenue, which must be visible with a good telescope? We can see things on their surface far smaller than that, and when the Earth is nearest to us its back is turned; still anything brilliant on the night side would be best seen then. If they had such a street we should know.

'The city has been laid off by mathematicians, and has been rebuilt hundreds of times. Its form is now finally settled; at least we think so, and communication with every part is perfect. Only the great main thoroughfares, those that cut the city into blocks of ten miles square, one hundred square miles, are right lines; the rest are curves of many different kinds. It was found that a constant succession of straight streets produced in some people a kind of insanity. With regard to the formation of streets and the structure of houses the rule now is endless variety.

'Our city is a huge garden; it is also a great orchard; millions of tons of vegetables are grown inside its boundaries. Its grain of various kinds has to come from outside as well as fish and preserved foods. Fowls are not permitted in the city except those of the air and of doves and songsters there are millions. None are imprisoned.

'There is no vehicular traffic in the streets. In spring and summer the open spaces are kept as parks and the footways are mostly like those I have mentioned as used in Port Howard and Granby. Here, however, the paths are wide and at least six of them run in parallel lines: with trees, shrubs and irregular little clumps of flower gardens between them. There is no noise in the streets and dust is a thing unknown. As the rainfall in this region is very slight irrigation has to take its place. For this purpose water has to be brought great distances but very little serves. We have not a hot sun drinking up every drop of moisture, and our plants are like our people in consuming very little water. I am told that on Earth man consumes more fluid than three Martials.

'There is a good deal of traffic by air boat. There are regular lines along the great avenues and streets; most of the boats will carry twenty passengers. There is also a great railway traffic. Stations are placed at every mile within fifty miles of the central square: this is the Urban Radius. Outside this the stations are two miles apart. Underneath the Grand and Central avenues there are four lines of railways, the central lines being for express traffic. The trains on the sidelines stop at every station; those running on the middle lines only stop at the ten-mile intersections.

'In order to get from the street to the railway line passengers have to step inside a double-railed space on the second footpath in the wide street. About every two minutes the inner railing and the portion of flooring it encloses descends and becomes part of the railway platform. Those going away walk off at one end while those coming up walk on at the other and then the platform becomes footpath once more. The outer railing is a guard to keep people from falling about thirty feet into the lower way.

'Travelling accounts with people are very easily kept. Persons wanting tickets by air boat or rail get them at the depot where they make their usual purchases and they go to the year's debit. In thousands of cases, I may say in millions, an annual ticket is issued for a man who has to make a certain journey twice daily, from home to work and back again. No attempts are ever made to defraud the traffic departments; if people were not above such trickery the old plan of paying coin would have to be resorted to. Mistakes are very rarely made with regard to the names of people; for with the name is given the section of the district in which you may reside. If there are two or three of a name they are known by a number.

'There is a great difference in the mode of getting supplies in the metropolis and in the rural districts such as I came from. There all we want is got from one depot; here the depots are much more numerous and each one has only a certain class of goods. Male clothing at one and female clothing at another; and we can go to any and get what we like from any after we are registered as responsible persons at the office for the purpose. Minors have to get their supplies through the head of the family. My badge will get me whatever I require anywhere, and at any time.

'The great railway lines are so constructed that lighting wires, speaking wires, water piping and drainage service can be carried on and each properly supervised by the men appointed; along most lines there is a pneumatic service also. By the use of the latter small articles can go from one end of the city to the other in an hour. At one time human beings wished to be shot along these tubes, but it was found that such rapid movement, although not felt, had an injurious effect, and it was therefore abolished. "Why so fast?" said our statesmen, and our movements were limited to the average rate of one hundred miles an hour. We all agree now that that is fast enough. There is no need to push through today as if there was no tomorrow. Our lives are happy and full of leisure because we gave up hurrying. The hurrying would have kept us in a constant fever, and nothing would have been gained by it. Five hours' work is pleasant and enables work that must go on constantly as, for instance, railway service, to be divided into five changes of men. In this metropolis, the trains run for passengers fifteen hours and ten hours during the night for goods; five changes of men are required.

'The Martial man is a very clean man and he makes no waste. The metropolitan district is dry, hence there is little need for drainage, but what little waste there is is removed during the day in which it occurs. Nothing that can make the air impure is allowed to remain a single day where it can do harm. Anything that can give off a smell is deodorised at once and removed and desiccated in a few hours. Dried sewerage is taken to the agricultural districts; not a single particle is wasted. No foul water is allowed to lodge for a day; every part of the surface of the land is kept clean. There is no dust in the streets, and they are made so pleasant that walking is a most agreeable and delightful exercise. Our young people think nothing of walking five or ten miles, for they are light and muscular, and there is no disagreeable heat or dust to annoy them. The railways and air boats are used more by elders and by those who have plenty of work without walking.

'We have very little disease and infant mortality is almost unknown even here where a thousand million people are brought together. The schools have ample space about them and are of every kind, and the recreation grounds – the breathing spaces – are well kept. The great aim in keeping them is to make them natural. Even in shape and size no two parks are alike.

'The government buildings occupy a block ten miles square. The Planetary Library has a mile of front to the

Grand Avenue and three miles to the Central Avenue. The College of Surgeons has a front of two miles, and many other buildings are quite a mile in length. The height of our buildings is three stories, and sometimes a perfect uniformity of structure will prevail for several miles. Very high buildings were at one time fashionable, but they seemed to shut out the day from the streets, and we found that their great shadows robbed vegetation of its colour and made the streets unpleasant to travellers.

'There are many hostels, and some of them are very great buildings. As is the case all over, they are owned by the government and the bills are charged to debit of annual accounts. The rank of hostel used has to correspond with the rank of worker. There is no attempt made to draw caste lines; indeed, the object of social life is to abolish them, but in spite of all that can be done the workers of certain ranks prefer to associate with their companions in labour. They are not at home with the workers of other ranks, who of necessity know more, and are more polite in demeanour. We are all altruistic socialists, all democrats; all either as individuals or as classes willing to waive our own rights in favour of others, and yet we cannot be equal. Andrew Grayson is not even "Sir" or "Esq." and yet he stands in the first rank, and all bow to him as a scholar in his line.

'The clerk in charge of our depot advised me to report myself at the Equatorial Hostel in the metropolis. It is the largest in existence. It has four stories and a basement, and has a solid stone front calculated to last a thousand years. There are ten thousand rooms in it and its corridors are traversed by some twenty miles of tram lines. It is always full, and the overflow of its residents fill several thousand rooms built in the rear, half a mile from the Grand Avenue, to which the main building has a mile of frontage. To describe this hostel with its fountains and gardens, its courts, gymnasium, music rooms, lecture hall, theatre, church, its suites of private rooms, its furniture, its balconies, its gardens and summer houses on the roof, is to describe a city in miniature. It is easy to spend years in it and not see half its beauties and advantages. Its rooms are all in communication with the entrance hall, and a visitor can instantly ascertain if the person he calls to see is at home.

'After getting at the museum the little information given above I entered my name at the Equatorial, and according to promise went to dine with Grayson. For the next year I will spend my time in the centre of the Great City. Five hours daily at the College of Engineers, some hours of leisure with the Grayson family. The rest of my time will probably be divided amongst the museums, libraries, art galleries, the Earthborn's Club and at the hostel, where I intend to sleep. I will write to my parents once a week, and I already begin to long for the company of Father, Mother, and my dear sister Emma.'

CHAPTER XIV

The Earthborn's Club

'ABOUT SIXTEEN O'CLOCK Grayson and I went to the home of the Earthborns. I was much surprised to find it a large building and to see, when we went into it, that there were so many people of both sexes there at that early hour. I thought that there could only be a few; what was my astonishment to find that this club had more than a thousand members, nearly half of whom were women of various ages. It appeared to me that there would not be much trouble in picking up the information Doctor Hildreth gave my mother on the day I overheard their conversation. Grayson had been away for a few weeks and as he went into room after room, the members rose to greet him; I did not know until then that he was president of the club. Really, in meeting this man at the very outset of my career, I was most fortunate. He is a power in the land; quiet, gentle and kind as he is, and willing to put up with so much in me that must appear very crude, raw and boyish. In four days I was fully elected a member of the club and had all the rights and advantages of that position.

'Here are people who are conscious, on Mars, of their Earth-life; others who are conscious on both sides; some who are conscious of Earth-life while on Earth and of Martial life while on Mars, but not, on either, conscious of the other. These are but few; there may be many, but for obvious reasons they are not easily discovered. One third are like me, living on both planets; the rest can give records of various periods. I was introduced to one woman who for twenty years had belonged to the club and who had been "transferred" but three days ago.

'I am very much impressed by a very commanding and handsome woman of about fifteen years of age. If royalty were a thing possible here I would call her a queen. I dare not attempt to describe her; she is not manly nor mannish and she associates on even terms with all of us but does not form any friendships. She appears to me to be a model of strength and gentleness; her eyes fascinate me and many others, and her voice has such a thrilling charm that most people are silent when she speaks.

'One evening we had a small musical gathering in the concert hall of the club. None but Earth songs had to be sung. She sang two that she called Scotch songs, written by one Burns, with such pathos that most of us shed tears, we were so deeply moved. One of our club members, a cheerful little man, gave us some comic songs, and others gave samples of the music and sentiment of Earth-dwellers from the time of Sophocles to that of Tom Moore. But the Scotch songs from Burns … those rang in my ears for days and weeks and led up to a closer acquaintance if not a friendship with Martha Newsome.

'In the club buildings there are two large rooms, one devoted to history and the other to geography of Earth.

In the geography chamber, the central object is a most perfectly finished globe, mounted so that it can be turned over in any direction with a mere touch. It is twelve feet in diameter and ruled in degrees of latitude and longitude, each tenth degree being indicated by a red line. There is not a town of any importance left off this globe and each town is correctly named, and on referring to the key, itself an encyclopedia of geography such as has never been produced on Earth, we find the small outlying villages belonging to the district named correctly. The mountains are raised in proportion to the size of the globe, and rivers and watersheds, lakes and inland seas are all in position. In addition to the great globe there are a number of smaller ones, from two to three feet in diameter; one of these is a copy of the original made and compiled before the "Black Century". This gives an antiquity of ten thousand Martial years, nearly nineteen thousand Earth years.

'In comparing this ancient globe with the modern ones I was astonished to find very little change in the geographical aspects, but there were great inhabited areas and large cities even at that time. A very vast population lived in Western America and all around the Mexican Gulf. Eastern Asia, India, Ceylon[14], Southern Asia and the valley of the Nile were covered with population a thousand years later. The pyramids of Egypt were built by the descendants of the men who built those in Arizona.

'My friend Martha told me that a peaceful nation had developed a high civilisation in Western America prior to the "Black Century", and that these people were driven across the Pacific by the constant incursions of wild tribes from the north and east of the American continent. She

---

14 Ceylon was a colonial name given to what is now known as Sri Lanka.

said, too, that vast hoards of gold, silver and precious stones are waiting to be unearthed from beneath the old pyramids of Arizona and other places in the south and west.

"If I wanted to write a history of our old home, indeed of our present home so far as we are concerned, I would come here for my materials. For all the records here are contemporaneous; men who knew related their own knowledge of facts actually transpiring at the time of relation," said she.

"I am sorry," said I, "that I know nothing of my other life. All I know is what I can remember of a brief half hour that Grayson kindly caused me to spend in Melbourne. Ignorant I am and can add nothing to these records, either historical or geographical."

"Do not let that matter trouble you," said Martha. "Your time will come, and if you can record nothing here you can write on the Earth side, and you are doing so. I, too, from my home in Edinbro', will make some communications, though my Scotch neighbours may think me mad. But it just strikes me that, situated as you are, there is a likelihood of your being ignorant of the differences between the inhabitants of these two planets."

"That is true," I answered. "I have only got a little vague information, and that only during my journey from the antipodes. I hoped to get that kind of knowledge here, but so far other matters have occupied my attention."

"Look at me," said Martha. "Do you think that I am as big as the woman whom you saw on Earth?"

"Yes, you appear about the same size or perhaps a little taller than the average."

"That is not the case," Martha replied. "If you had met me in the streets of Melbourne in my present form you would have seen a sharp, thin little dwarf, about three feet ten inches in height and very slight, about half the weight of an ordinary Earth-woman. If you had met me in Edinbro' you would have seen a strong woman of middle age, about five feet seven inches in height. There I am the mother of four fine sons and two daughters and I cannot make either my husband or any member of my family thoroughly understand my position. I live a very active life in my Earth-home and am a happy woman. I do not know by what dispensation I am allowed to have two bodies and two lives. How one soul animates two bodies I cannot tell; my mental faculties are equally on the alert in both spheres. On Earth I worship in the Church of Scotland; here I attend Thanksgiving every Sabbath morning. I am equally happy in the two kinds of worship. I might have married here, have had to refuse several offers, but for the fact that my Earth-life is so present and real that I should feel as if guilty of bigamy. My husband in Edinbro' is a good man, but he is not a Martial, or if he is, he knows nothing about it. It seems as if there is something more in man than body and soul. John Wesley[15] was perhaps right in speaking of body, spirit and soul."

"This difference in height and size must involve a number of differences. A given number of Martials will consume

---

15 Evangelical cleric John Wesley (1703–1791) led a revival within the Church of England that eventually became the Protestant nonconformist religion known as 'Methodism', and which promoted a model of Christian conversion driven by intense personal experience. With its surging music, promise of salvation and liberal politics, Wesleyan Methodism became a major religion in colonial Australia and Aotearoa New Zealand. The Frasers maintained close ties to the denomination, even though Fraser also posited an alternative religious philosophy in his 1880 lecture titled *The Religion of Phrenology* (Auckland: Wilsons & Horton).

far less food than the same number of Earth-dwellers, and I have previously known that they will consume less fluid?"

"Yes," said Martha, "the Earth-man will eat three times as much food, and in many cases five times as much, and he has to take more fluid to make up for fluid waste. Sometimes, indeed, he drinks for the sake of drinking and dies a victim to what is unknown here, the vice of drunkenness. We may say that, on the average, what will support one Earth-man would support four of our people. We have to remember that the Earth-man has to lift a body twice as cumbrous and to stand the pull of twice as much gravitation, so that in making any movement he has four times the work to do that we have. He has also to stand the pressure of a much heavier atmosphere."

"You, being conscious on both sides, see all this, I suppose?"

"Indeed, no, I do not," said Martha. "I have had to learn it. In coming from one planet to the other I perceive none of these differences. Everything is in proportion in both, so that nothing strikes us as different. We must, however, in reading and writing about the two planets, remember that there are several differences, or we may make mistakes. They could not be serious ones after all. A few errors of size and distance would not invalidate the general truth of what we write and say. Our Central Avenue is a thousand miles to us, and if an Earth-man came it would be the same to him if he came as we came, the only way possible, but if he could bring his Earth faculties it would be about three hundred and forty miles, still a fairly long street. He might find out that our foot is not twelve inches, but only eight; but before he could live our life with us it would be a foot again. We have only four-ninths of the heat and light of the sun that the Earth-people have, but here we are used

to what we have and should not be able to stand a change
to Earth conditions any more than an Earth-man could
stand a change to ours. Our Maker has wisely adapted us
to the circumstances and surroundings of our life, and we
have been wise enough to make the best of these also. We
live only by following out the Divine plan and obeying the
laws of our being."

"We must be weak as compared with the Earth-men!"

"No," said my friend, "considering our size we are a
strong and compact species. We are relatively stronger and
more active than our Earth friends and we are warmer
and our death rate is much lower. We do not employ half
so many surgeons and physicians as they do. Our work is
done more easily, but we are a busy race and have twice
as many workers in proportion, profitable people as they
have. Indeed, as you have already seen, this is for the
greater part a made world; an idle population could not
live upon it. We work to a purpose here. Our time is not
spent in making guns, building forts and ships of war,
and standing, millions of us, waiting to kill each other at
the word of command. Again, we have not a vast population who spend their time in buying, selling and carrying
about all kinds of provisions and goods. What we make
goes direct to the consumer and pays him for his work.
The middle man who buys from the manufacturer and
sells to the consumer and makes a profit out of articles
that are not better but frequently worse for going through
his hands does not exist here. This sets at liberty a whole
army of men for industrial and productive pursuits."

"But these changes will gradually be made upon Earth?"

"Eventually they will," answered Martha, "though not yet.
Earth-dwellers are not yet ready for an altruistic socialism.

Their actions are selfish; they wish to acquire and to hold for themselves. We seek for the good of others and know that they seek for ours. On Earth, people have to lock all their doors; here, we have no need for lock or key. We only close doors and windows to keep out the cold; they have to use hasp and bolt and lock to keep out thieves. True, there is no incentive to steal or to accumulate, for we can always obtain what we require as long as we live. We cannot fall into poverty, and if by any chance we should become possessed of more wealth of any kind than we can use it would have to go into the coffers of the State."

"The State, it appears to me, holds all the wealth."

"Practically it does," was the reply. "Who could hold it so safely and distribute it so wisely? Besides, the State is the people; we have a perfect democracy and a perfect socialism. No class can prey upon any other class in social life; all are free and have equal rights. We cannot be equal in power and capacity, hence some are greater than others. Politically we are self-governed and all laws are made for the benefit of all."

"But our laws are not made by the people and for them?"

"By whom, then, are they made and for whom?" asked my fair instructor. "The Central Executive of one hundred of the best and most capable men and women on our planet meets twice a week not far from here for the purpose of directing the affairs of the world and for the good of all its dwellers, but that body cannot make a law; it can only put laws into operation. When a same new law is wanted, men and women selected by the people form a temporary Parliament and consider the question. These are rare occasions. The Central itself when it wants a new member elects one from those selected in each district to manage local affairs."

"Power must be invested somewhere?"

"It must," answered Martha, "and on Mars it is held by those who cannot be interested in abusing it. We have no party. Whosoever joins the Central is elected for life and has no advantage but that which you hold, viz. the Freedom of the Planet. We are not ruled by a mob, nor by a despot. We rule ourselves and make the wise one hundred administrators of the laws we have from time to time made."

"I have had very little experience of life except that which I have lived here as a Martial youth. I know practically nothing of Earth-life. I am therefore to be excused if I ask you what you think of the moral tone of the Earthborns who come to this planet. Are they equal to the people of Mars?"

"Generally they are," answered Martha. "If they were not fit to associate with the Martials they would not be born here. Without flattering ourselves we may say that we have risen to another world. Your Earth-life has been pretty good, else you would not have been here. It is possible that some of us are prepared for Martial life by the influence of friends on Mars. There may be much more connection than we dream of between the two planets. Most of what you regard as new inventions are Martial suggestions received from the souls of friends who have come to dwell in a smaller but happier, better world. Some of our Earth-friends may be tempted more than the Martials are, but I have never heard of anything being done by an Earthborn that might not have been done by a Martial."

"You remember the Earth-life and I do not. Can you tell me if there are any people there who claim to be from Venus?"

"I can," answered my friend. "There are none. Venus may be a grand world some day. It will be able to support life when the sun has left us in the cold, but it is one hundred thousand years short of the human stage at present. It is passing through a carboniferous epoch and its highest life is that of reptiles. It is fourteen times as hot as it is here and it receives light in like proportion, but the light will never reach the surface of the planet through the thick, heavy atmosphere."

'At this point my friend left me, having some other matter to attend to and a young man who had heard some of our conversation told me that she had come to study music for a year at the great school. He was afraid that she was not very happy as she did not appear to form social ties of any kind. He was interested in our conversation because he, like me, knew nothing about his Earth-life. He said that he was studying Earth history and found great pleasure in it because it corresponded in many ways with that of our own planet in its early days. He discovered that there had been a time when tribe fought against tribe and later a time when nation fought against nation in the history of our own world, and he thought that the Earth was developing and growing and only going through the experiences that belonged to its period of evolution.

"I can trust the records I find here," said the youth, "for they are fresh and are corroborated by many observers. Look at the commonplace journal, in which each Earth-man, who is conscious on the Earth side, records the principal events of his day. One says that a German statesman, Bismarck, and the present emperor of Germany are trying to ameliorate the condition of the working classes; that the statesman is devising a plan to prevent the artisans from falling into poverty. Read entries made by other Europeans of our Club and you find that they all allude to it. No less than three Americans tell us that a millionaire, Carnegie, of Pittsburg, says that his class ought to invest their millions for the public good during life, and above all things not to leave wealth to their children. He would make the State heir of half his wealth. This is a step towards making the State sole heir as with us. And now, for the last ten days, we have been receiving accounts, from some hundred or more, of a great revolt of labourers in London and of the sympathy their revolt has excited in all parts of the British Empire. One of our recorders, writing of your city of Melbourne, says that the little colony, having in it only about twice as many people as the strikers and their families, has sent twenty-two thousands of pounds to the relief of the sufferers by the strike. Look at the significance of those three events. They all tell of the growth of altruism both in the Christian Church, where it is supposed specially to reside, and in the larger world of men, who are beginning to recognise the tie which binds each man to all his fellow men. In a thousand years hence these records of Earth history will be invaluable, and we can rely on their truth because if false they would be contradicted now."

'I was almost startled by this outburst from so young a man and began to think his company worth more than I at first supposed, and I therefore exchanged cards with him. "George Foster" was on his card. I asked him if he knew his Earth name. He answered that he did, and he mentioned a name known as that of a statesman, a scholar and a historian all the Earth over. I no longer wondered. I knew that such a shining soul must attain to greatness even in Mars.

'This day I spent the evening at Grayson's. His wife is a sweet-voiced gentle matron, with hair as white as his own. Their family of three children are all married; the younger daughter and her husband live with the old people and keep the house alive. Mother Grayson treats me with the utmost kindness. She tries to make her house a home for me. She has a place for my books and has a comfortable corner of her sitting room, with chair and table, set apart for me. This evening, Grayson asked me if I was willing to forego the pleasure and profit of my course of studies at the College of Engineers for about half a year.

'I answered, expressing my willingness to do so if any good end could be served thereby.

"That being the case," said he, "you will receive an intimation from the Central after its next meeting. The Minister of Agriculture has decided to make a trial of your discovery and invention on a moderately large scale during the next spring and summer. He is therefore preparing to lay tubes and wires in a piece of land five miles square, now inside the snow line. The land gets free from snow and ice in summer and rapidly grows a lot of grass, and even a crop of tubers is sometimes grown. But we cannot trust the land, and unless a crop can be got in very early, it cannot be ripened and secured."

"The Central, then," I asked, "wishes me to clear this twenty-five miles of land and apply electrical warmth?"

"Yes," said Grayson, "the men and the materials are already there: two engineers are also directing operations. You are wanted to supervise the special part with which you are most familiar, so that the experiment may have a fair chance."

'I now know for the first time that Grayson is a member of that august body, the Central Executive.'

CHAPTER XV

In the North

'As I expected, I received a note from the Secretary of the Central asking me if I could make it convenient to supervise the subwarming of a strip of level and pretty good land twenty miles in length, from east to west, and five in width, from north to south. I had not to consider myself bound to go, and I was to have a special swift air boat to take me to and from as often as I chose.

'I at once and gladly accepted the commission, knowing that I could at any time go on with my studies at the College.

'I wrote Mother and Father asking them to defer for a little while their visit to Sidonia and next day found me rapidly flying to the north. I took with me Fred Harley, an aspiring young engineer, who had completed his college course and wanted to make himself useful. For several weeks I directed the operations of the staff of men employed and had the satisfaction of making a practical test. For a late snowstorm came and covered my completed work and suspended operations in other parts. I turned on my heat and had the satisfaction of seeing the snow melt and the land grow green, while all around was locked up in a wintry sleep.

'Sometimes Harley and I would go about twenty miles of a flight up the snow farther north, partly for pleasure and partly to see whether or not we could extend operations. We would have taken longer flights had our boat been fitted to carry more stores of force. As it was, we on one occasion went too far and had to walk home over the snow, sometimes through it. Our boat had to be carried five miles next day. We also had a sleigh, but the snow surface was broken up too much and we could not make much use of it.

'Government boats, specially equipped, have been at the north and south poles. The snowcaps, however, are very great. They extend for twenty degrees of latitude even in summer, and in winter they come twenty degrees further. Indeed, the subsoil is almost always frozen above the fiftieth parallel of latitude. Winter begins to be felt as positive cold at thirty degrees from the equator, ice and snow forming in great quantities.

'I had almost finished my task and was thinking of returning to Sidonia, pushing on with my studies, and of the pleasure of going to all the grand sights of the metropolis with Father, Mother and Sister, when one night something happened to modify my plans.

'It was about twenty-three o'clock, and I was just about to retire, when Fred Harley came running in with the news that an air boat with three people in it was supposed to be lost on the snowfields.

'We had two air boats and a sleigh at our disposal and I requested Harley to charge all the accumulators while I got particulars. I found that a boat containing three travellers had called about seventy-five minutes, three-quarters of an hour ago. It was going to the village of Ayreton, eighty miles to the west, and would have to call at the next station to renew its electrical supply in about thirty minutes. In such cases it was usual to report arrival. The report had not come and the man in charge had seen nothing of the boat. It was already half-an-hour behind time and its route lay over a desolate snowfield with an atmospheric temperature below zero. The boat would not have warning appliances; it was described as a common family one.

'The large boat was ready when I got back and I left Fred to make ready for the starved strangers if I could find them. I turned the light into a couple of search lamps that Fred had attached, and flying as low as I dared went after the missing ones. I had travelled quite twenty miles when I saw something dark on the snow surface and went down to see if it was anything dropped from the missing boat. Truly it was something dropped; the dark object was the covering of a woman's head. She was all but buried in loose, powdery, dry snow, and could not have extricated herself. If I had not had the good fortune to find her she would soon have perished. When I attempted to lift her out of the drift into my boat she made some effort to send me away in search of her father and brother, who were in some difficulty further on. Evidently she wanted me to leave her.

'This I could not do. I lifted her up and wrapped her in a rug, and went forward on the track of the missing boat. In another fifteen minutes I found it. It was disabled owing to an accident. The old man, feeling down in the bottom of the boat for something in the dark, had mistaken his position and accidentally slipped his hand in the joint or hinge of the propeller. It had, of course, smashed his hand, and even his wrist, and the jerk had thrown his daughter out. For some time neither father nor son knew that anything had happened to the girl; they were busy, the son in trying to bind up the hand, the father in bearing his pain. When the loss was discovered they flew back and round, about and across and across their track until their supply of power gave out and they dropped helplessly to the ground.

'There was nothing before these two also but death before morning. It was very fortunate that I had taken the larger boat, for I took them on board and calculating how far I had come decided to go forward as it would be nearer than going back. In a few minutes more we were at the station and could see each other and look at the wounded hand. It was very badly injured. All we could do was to bind it up and stop the bleeding. There was no help to be had there, and if they had come back with me I could not have done much more for them, so we went to Ayreton. It was fifty miles due west, but mine being a first-class boat and fully charged cleared the distance in less than half an hour.

'After I got to Ayreton I meant to return, but was persuaded to remain. This was not a very difficult task for I had told Fred that I might not come back and I was a little interested in the family and desired to know more about its members – especially one of them.

'When first I heard this girl speak her voice had a strange thrill that seemed to run through me and I knew not what memories. I wanted to hear her speak again and yet again and each time she spoke the same sensation stole over or through me. I felt that the voice had something to say to me and that no other voice could say it. I could not define the effect. I could not tell in what it differed from other voices, but it had a charm for me. I cannot be in love. I have only heard her speak a few times. I have never had a conversation with her, I have never looked fairly into her face. I know nothing of her and yet her voice runs through me and keeps ringing in my brain.

'The first thing I listen for in the morning is that voice, and hearing it amongst others at a distance the same feeling comes over me again. Had I not better go? Why should I stay to see her? I can be back at my work in less than an hour, why wait? And yet I wait and as I look upon her from my window I can see that she is certainly looking for me. Perhaps I had better let her have the opportunity of thanking me for the little service I rendered them. Besides, it would be cruel to go away without enquiring about the old man's hand. He must have had a terrible night of pain with that smashed member. Does fate hang on these little things?

"Good morning, Helen, I hope you are not injured by the severe experiences last evening." These commonplace words I managed to get out someway and then I became silent. I had approached to within a few feet of her and got the first glance of her eye and the first fair look at her face. So far she had not spoken, but she just glanced at me and her eyes dropped and her face changed colour.

"Thank you, I am quite well. We have all to thank you that we are not dead in the snow this morning. Father is in great trouble and pain. Doctor Simmons is with him and she says he will have to undergo amputation, some of the bones in the wrist being completely pulverised."

'While speaking about her father, she became quite natural again and looked a very pleasant, winsome and happy girl of about nine years of age. The Martial women are all beautiful and well-proportioned. To say that Helen Vance is beautiful is but to utter a platitude. She is fair, her eyes are blue, her hair has plenty of golden sunshine in it; not red, but rich gold, fine, bright and full of rippling wavelets and curly masses.

'Her eye is a puzzle to me. It seems to be looking at something far away in the distance one moment and the next it has a deep pleading beauty like that seen in some well-bred and superior animals. I have seen it before and I have heard that voice before sometime, somewhere. Bodily she may be a stranger to me, but there is something familiar in those two great soul revealers: the eye and the voice.

"Is your father unwilling to have the hand removed? It may be a question of life and death in a few days, perhaps hours. He must be already much weakened through the shock and what he has suffered since."

"Quite true, but he thinks that if he could get to the metropolis early he might have the powdered bones taken out and replaced with silver. There are such wonders in surgery performed in these days."

"We can have him in the metropolis in two days or very little more if that is all. I can take you and your father and Fred Harley can bring your brother, but we cannot travel night and day at this season of the year. We cannot go much more than a thousand miles a day."

"How kind you are," said Helen. "Our own boat might be made to serve, however. My brother says it is not disabled; that it only had to stop because its power was spent. If you would let my brother have your boat he could half fill our accumulators and bring both back, one at once. We then could return as we came."

'I did not relish this idea. I wanted to take the sufferer and his daughter myself. I could send for Fred to help with the boat.

"Perhaps I had better see your father. Mine is a new government boat and very powerful. If your father and you can bear to travel in the night I will have you in Sidonia, in the metropolitan hospital, in thirty hours or less."

"Oh, that will be best," said Helen. "Do see him before the doctor goes. I will go first and tell them of your readiness and ability to help. I can travel in the night if father can, and maybe we will start at once."

'A moment later Helen called me into her father's room and the doctor, who for the present had given up the idea of persuading her patient to undergo an amputation, asked me a few questions. For a moment she seemed inclined to treat me as a very young man, but her manner changed when she saw the badge. She said, "I am sorry to have to tell you, Frankston, that you are undertaking a very difficult if not a dangerous task. I advise an immediate start. The nerve shock and the intense pain have almost brought on collapse. I dare not make free use of sedatives under the circumstances. Hern must be kept still and well wrapped. You will be in a warmer latitude tonight and so may travel right on. Still, taking what care you may I cannot guarantee that he will reach Sidonia alive."

'I had sent for Fred half-an-hour before, and as he had only eighty miles to come I knew he might be expected any minute. And before we had got Thomas Hern comfortably settled he was at hand. I introduced him to Henry Hern, Helen Vance's brother, and left the two to bring on the boats to Sidonia. I told them my route and advised them to follow it so that if anything happened they would know in a few minutes.

'Away I went, up into the space above all law, and then bearing south-west by south, I shot along at the rate of one hundred and fifty miles an hour. I had to recharge at each hundred miles – what a pity we cannot carry an indefinite supply of electricity. I will invent some plan. At seventeen o'clock we had travelled a thousand miles. If I could keep up the same speed, during the night we should be in Sidonia before daylight and at the hospital by ten o'clock, twenty-six hours after starting.

'We were now travelling over a populous district almost town-like in the number of its inhabitants to the square mile. I dropped in a small village and got a recharge and some refreshments, for in our haste we had forgotten our usual meal, and we knew that our strength would be wanted during the night. Our patient was asleep, and to all appearance doing well, so we soon shot off again. I could not now fly quite so high and so quickly, for I had to keep an eye upon the lights below that tell of charging places. At our next drop I found that Fred Harley and Harry Hern were following, and that the boats were all right. I told them where we were and reported "All well." After this I spoke to them twice more.

'When I alighted a third time, however, and was filling up with power, I heard a wild cry of grief and pain break the silence of the night. I flung down my insulators and went astern to see what was the matter, and there found Helen thrown full length on the dead body of her father. The man had passed away in his sleep without a word or sign. Only the coldness of his face under its loose covering told her what had happened.

'As a rule, the Martials do not fear death and do not make much of it. They never wear mourning and never indulge in a grand funeral. This girl was a very affectionate one and had been her father's favourite from birth, and so the sudden loss was a terrible affliction. I did not try to check her tears: I knew that they would bring relief, and so merely got her away from her father's body. I communicated with her brother and Fred and went to the nearest hostel for the night. I gave Helen up to the matron, who was very kind and sympathetic, and left the body laid out in the boat until Harry and Fred could arrive.

'It was morning when they came. They were weary and had forgotten to take dinner the day before. I saw that they had breakfast and we all rested until noon. We then decided to take the old man's body to his home. Harry sent word to Mother Vance. Fred and Harry went in Hern's boat and I carried Helen and the corpse. We were a silent company. We had to go to Highton, section 725, a district some three hundred miles north-east of Sidonia. We arrived at nineteen o'clock and found all in readiness for our burden. Fred and I were invited to remain with the family, but thinking they would be better without us we went to the hostel.

'The next day, at noon, a special boat with a receptacle for the corpse came to Hern's. We were ready to follow it. A married sister of Helen's and her husband, Mother Vance, Helen, Harry, Fred and I followed in three boats. We flew slowly to the nearest crematory.

'There we alighted on a beautifully kept lawn, and four men came for the corpse. It was carried into the building and placed on a kind of shelf near one of the walls. There was nothing about the building that we could see to suggest fire or death or anything painful or unpleasant. We followed the body in, and each placed upon it a stick of perfumed wood and a few flowers. Then one of our religious teachers, a friend of the family, came and made a few appropriate remarks, mostly of a consoling and thanksgiving character. What he said ended in something like this strain: "The untenanted body of our friend who has passed from amongst us we reverently commit to the elements from whence it has been derived. It was to him a clothing and a useful working servant. He treated it properly as a gift of God. He has left it for us to dispose of and we set its various component parts free that they may again be of use in other structures. This is not our friend whom we return to nature's storehouse, but a shell that he has worn and done with. Our friend is in God's hands, and is therefore safe. Nothing evil can happen to him, for the Giver of Life gave Death as the end of Life, its natural conclusion, and what is natural is also right and good."

'Here the speaker pressed a spring and the shelf and its burden slowly drew into the wall. As it went he said: "What we have known as Thomas Hern passes from our sight forever. The real man is as real as ever and is working out his destiny of eternal progress to better and better states of being."

'We then stood in silence for a few minutes and went our various ways.

'I spent the remainder of the day in Highton, and made friends of Mother Vance and Henry. I saw little of Helen, but was probably more interested in her on that account. Her voice, whenever I heard it, rang through my brain as before, and as I shook hands with her next morning I got one glance of her strange, deep, dumb pleading eye that I could never forget.

'Fred and I returned to Sidonia. I promised to see the Herns in the Autumn. When I got back to Sidonia I received a complimentary letter from the Central Executive.

'One of my first acts was to tell Grayson of my adventures. He listened with pleasure and attention. When I spoke of Helen Vance he looked grave and troubled, especially when I told him of the strange effect of her eye and voice.

'The next day he told me that he had discovered Helen was an Earthborn, and frequently, though not constantly, conscious of her Earth-life. She would be eligible shortly to become a member of the "Earthborn." He also said that I had possibly seen her before.'

From this time to the end of the sixty-fifth of our diarist's Earth-years there is nothing of importance recorded in either life. Frankston goes on with his studies in Mars, and Jacobs with his commission agencies in Melbourne. Occasionally he speaks of his wife as ailing, and evidently business is not prosperous on his side. His wife and sons have had something better in hand than he has.

Near the end of seventy-nine he writes: 'My greatest bereavement has fallen upon me. My wife is dead. For forty years we have travelled the world together and we have been faithful to each other all the time. Our love was a quiet current on which our lives floated: it has taken death to show me how deep and strong that current is. I had no idea that I could suffer so much. My only hope is that we may meet again; eternity will be an empty void without her. In anguish of soul I cry out for my lost love.'

His loss must have stirred him to the depths of his soul before he left the matter-of-fact style used so far.

His notes for the next two years are very prosy and mixed up much with business transactions. Sometimes there is not a word from Mars for days together. His double is living quietly and happily. He has the friendship of many good and wise people. He sees Helen Vance now and then. She has become a member of the Earthborn's Club and is working in the metropolis. His family have spent some time in Sidonia and have seen some of the sights there only to be seen. As for seeing them, all that is out of the question; even a Martial lifetime would not suffice for that. Doctor Edith Somers continues to take an interest in him and his practical answer to Croakers. Several more areas are being redeemed from the snowfields in the north and he goes now and then to spend a week in supervision. The reclaimed lands are much sought after and are very productive, the soil being new. He continues to spend afternoons and evenings frequently with the Graysons. He is now in his twelfth year and has fully decided to make Sidonia his home. This partly because he likes metropolitan life and partly because, when there, he is in communication with the Central Executive. He is always progressing in knowledge and likes to remain in touch with the leaders of thought and action in the centre of his world.

We now return to the diary.

CHAPTER XVI

LIFE IN SIDONIA. CONSCIOUSNESS

'YOU THINK, THEN, that you could enjoy life in the Great City?'

'I certainly could. It appears to be ever more and more interesting, I have no desire to return to Highton.'

The speakers are Charles Frankston and Helen Vance. They are taking an afternoon walk along the Grand Avenue. Hundreds more are indulging in the same kind of recreation. The springy, silent footpaths enable them to move without clatter. The green aisles stretch an illimitable vista before them, broken by shrubs and clumps of sweet smelling and radiant flowers. Mars is a paradise of colour. The colour rays are very abundant in the subdued sunlight, and the heat rays and chemical rays are not strong enough to destroy colours. There are little avenues of trees here and there also, but nothing is carried far enough to become monotonous.

Our young folks walk along a happy and well-matched pair, so pleasant to look upon and so friendly and happy in each other's company that many of those passing to and fro, many who know them and meet them with nods and smiles and pleasant greetings, are compelled to turn and give them a second glance.

'It is my intention,' said Charles, 'to make this my home. For one thing, all that takes place in any part of our planet is at once known here, and for another, what operations I have going on can be easily controlled from here. I have reclaimed from the snowfields more than a thousand square miles.'

'Why do you not do the same for the south as for the north?' asked Helen.

'Probably that will come about in good time. At present, however, there is no hurry; and further, the south is better off than the north, for being nearer the sun in summer it gets about ten per cent more fine days than the northern hemisphere has. Somehow or other our population is denser in the north also.'

'Is the warming plan turning out a success in the temperate regions where it is being tried?'

'For some growths, yes, for others the answer is yet scarcely available. Tubers, esculents and ground fruits, berries of various kinds are much increased, the increase paying the cost of laying wires and pipes in about three seasons.'

'You were speaking the other night about going to the Observatory some evening,' said Helen. 'Harry and I would take a great delight in looking at my old home.'

'Ah, yes! The home you left a thousand days ago. How strange that you, so young and fresh and fair—'

'There, there. That is enough for the present.'

'Yes. But seriously, how strange that you should have undergone death, as they term it, down there, and should be here so full of life and ministering to the happiness of all of us.'

'Leave compliments. It is our universal duty to minister to happiness, as you term it. Did I not run the risk of passing away here before dying on Earth, a thing that has happened to many? Where would my lot have been cast this bright afternoon if your boat had not been available that memorable night?'

'Well, well. We'll cry quits and go on trying to make everybody happy; that is, if there is anything to add to the cup of human happiness. I ask for something more, and yet I ought to be content. I love the north for the friends it gave me and sometimes hope that—'

'Oh dear, you are spoiling the afternoon by being too sentimental. Let us change the subject. How soon may we expect to see sister Emma again?'

'You are commissioned to ask that question, I suppose?'

'Well, if I am, what then?' said Helen, archly. 'That brother of mine is a tease.'

'I wish I had a brother who would negotiate as you do for yours.'

'Poor fellow. What will you wish for next? You might find a brother inconvenient. He would probably negotiate for himself. Be thankful you have a sister and please answer my question.'

'I will since you seem in earnest about it. I phoned them this morning. Mother, Father and Sister will all be here in fifteen days and I am full of the most pleasant anticipations regarding their visit.'

'I suppose you are going to enjoy a little of the long-promised leisure you have spoken of for more than a year? Considering that you are free of the planet and can please yourself whether you ever do anything more or not, you seem to me to work a good deal.'

'Perhaps the "Freedom" may mean freedom to work. I take it as such and I am sure that if I sank into a state of ignoble idleness and self-indulgence you would be the first to condemn me. Look at Grayson, he has the badge and he works as hard as ever spite his fifty years.'

'That is all very well,' said Helen, 'but you know what all work and no play means. Generally we have plenty of play here, and surely when our modicum of work is finished we may play without feeling that any moral law is thereby infringed. Just look over our day's programme. At the club this afternoon we have a lecture on "prehistoric history" of the Earth. Our friend Phillips is going to people again those Asiatic cities that were full of life when the world was young. Then tonight we have one of Shakespeare's plays, *A Midsummer Night's Dream*. I will not miss that. At the Equatorial you have an opera and there are about two hundred other entertainments inside the urban radius, all for tonight. We are fond of amusements and a fair modicum of instruction, and who can say that we are less happy or less virtuous on that account?'

'I am afraid that we push amusement too far and that we are in danger of making our lives a little too empty. Too much play is as bad as too much work.'

'Well, you are in no danger anyway. Too much play has not hurt you so far.'

'I grant that,' said Charles, 'and it is really my intention to share in a grand excursion up the Sidon. I invite you and your brother. My father and Emma will go, and perhaps Mother.'

'Oh, well, you know Harry will go wherever there is a chance of Emma's company. As for me, I will stay at home and keep Mother company. There will be plenty of you for a very nice party.'

Helen went on with this kind of conversation for some time, showing how well they could enjoy themselves, and picturing herself at home helping Mother and doing up some neglected duties and attending to some studies that had fallen a little behind. She pretended not to see the look of absolute distress that pained the face of her companion.

'I shall be very sorry if you cannot go,' said Charles. 'Your absence will take all the brightness out of the trip. You see, we have been companions and friends so long. I have grown quite used to you. It is strange that a similar feeling has not sprung up in you.'

'Oh, well, we'll see what Mother says; perhaps she will spare me. At any rate, you can count upon me for a visit to the Observatory. We will turn back now, if you please, and go to the club. I want to read the Shakespearian play before seeing the performance tonight.'

'May I have the pleasure of accompanying you to the play tonight?'

'Of course you can come,' replied Helen. 'Who is to hinder you? Your membership entitles you and even your medal would pass you. I am going to strain my privilege and take with me a poor young man who has neither of your advantages. Fred Harley is about to be introduced to our great Earth Poet tonight.'

'Well, Fred is a good fellow and I am glad to see that you interest yourself in his welfare. He has only a few days in town. He has entered heart and soul into helping on my work. I have given him the position of Chief Engineer on the Humbrian Plains contract. It will occupy him, his staff and cadets and some two hundred men for five years. It is highly probable that he will obtain the Badge at the end of that term if his work is thoroughly well performed, and it will be. He has already obtained a very important concession. The ministers of railways, air boats and sea boats have each given him a Life Pass, so he may travel how he likes, and his journeys will never be charged against his labour.'

'I am pleased to hear that,' said Helen. 'How pleasant it is to live under a government that recognises services and gives rewards. In the world we come from, all they have learned to give is a pension or a title. More frequently the latter than the former. The highest of these is a new name and a seat in an obsolete parliament. Some men get a lot of titles; so many that they seem to drag the alphabet after their names.'

'Yes, and there is another vast difference. On Earth there is no authority that can grant anything equal to that which Fred now has, much less what he will have by-and-by. Speaking of Earth, do you remember much of it? You rarely mention it to me. To hear you name it is a new sensation, and yet you were conscious of the dual life all the time.'

'Conscious on this side, not on the other. My condition was just the reverse of yours. On Earth I knew nothing of Mars.'

'You were married and lived a long life there. I have been told that you were over sixty and had a family and that your husband is still alive.'

'All that is true, but you will excuse me if I do not at present talk about it. I have found it best since childhood never to let the lives mix. I do not think much about my Earth-life. I believe it was a school or a nursery of a hard sort and that to be born here is a promotion. I have several reasons for not saying much; you will find out some of them when you gain consciousness – but here we are – good afternoon.'

'I will not trouble you tonight. I wish our mutual friend Fred to spend a really enjoyable evening and that he is sure to do it with you.'

'Oh, how kind. Have you any more like that? Ta-ta, till we meet again.'

Sidonian life is evidently a pleasant thing, going by the peeps of it that we get from these diaries. No need to lock a door; all amusements free to all. No class distinction in evening or afternoon gatherings or in public worship. No dust, no heat, no noise nor jar. No grinding toil, no anxiety regarding business, no money, no poverty, no burdensome riches; plenty for all and all nearly as free as water or air. No demands to meet except twenty hours a week of labour and that itself is so much a privilege that those to whom it was denied owing to mental or physical incapacity are the only sufferers, or nearly so. Women and men are free and equal; a woman does not resign her name or any social right. She has her voice in selecting a representative for either District or Central Executives and from within that body her vote in selecting the most suitable from the selected. Nothing but disablement or transference can remove a member, hence the best three are selected and one elected for a council wants some voice in picking men whom it cannot send away.

The fifth day is the Sabbath and every kind of work stops, that can by any possibility be allowed to stop, so that the people can attend morning Thanksgiving and be free to spend the day as they please. They do not travel that day except on foot or by private air boat because they will not partake of any pleasure that deprives another of his chance of enjoying the same. They cannot endure the picture of one man working for the gratification of two or three more. Still, this altruism works two ways: any man if asked would work for the benefit of the rest or even to minister to others' pleasure.

The religious life of the community is free from sectarianism and free from cant. Little is said regarding the ten commandments, but the eleventh is always obeyed. No one will wrong another. The religious faith may best be defined as a pure Theism and the worship is mostly musical and full of praise and thanksgiving. It is entered into by all with great heartiness. In summer, and even in winter if the weather is fine and dry, worship is conducted in amphitheatres. One near the junction of the avenues will seat twenty-five thousand people and when used it is filled. An orchestra of two hundred performers is backed up by a trained choir of a thousand voices, and in the parts of the service that allows of both priest and people speaking in unison the effect is overwhelming.

At least Frankston so defines it. Says he: 'My little village ideas were all set adrift. When I got through a long, wide passage at the level of the street I found myself with about three or four thousand more people at one end of a great oval. The other half of the oval was occupied by a high platform for a reader. He was near the centre of the vast assemblage. Looking up on both sides I saw seven galleries separated from each other by broad, shallow flights of steps. One gallery was opposite the priest and would seat four thousand people. Then there were three more on each side capable of holding each three thousand more. In the oval where I was, there were no seats but four thousand could stand comfortably.

'I went in to see one of the Sabbath morning sights of Sidonia, and up to this time I had not regarded public worship as a thing of much account. I had been inside the walls about three minutes when I saw the man in the high reading desk stand up and place an open book before him. I then felt the whole audience, as it were, getting itself ready for an effort. All the musicians that I could see were in position and ready. Then the minister touched a gong and twenty-two thousand people rose as a cloud, and the orchestra broke into music and the choir and congregation burst into a jubilant song, beginning,

"We Praise Thee, O God.

We thank Thee, Giver of All Good."

'From this moment, for an hour and a half (fifty minutes) I was carried beyond myself. I felt as if I could have all but burst with joyful cries. I have never missed a service of the kind since. When it was over each line of spectators divided in the middle and walked off quickly each way. As one line went the next above it rose. Glancing round I saw that the same thing was going on in each gallery, and that the broad steps were never crowded, and that no one pushed against anyone else or moved with indecorous haste. In less than ten of our little minutes, twenty-five thousand people had got into the streets. Where there is a population of one thousand millions there are crowds now and then.'

The information above given is gathered from many pages of our diary.

A few more days have passed. Harley has gone to his work. Thomas Frankston and Mary and Emma Vaughan, Charlie's mother and sister, have taken up their quarters at the Equatorial. Harry Hern can scarcely be found anywhere else. Next second day, a party of five go for a grand tour to see more of the Great City. Mother Vaughan has decided to remain and keep Mother Vance company, so that the party will now consist of five most congenial spirits. They are: Thomas and Charles Frankston, father and son, but more like brothers; Harry Hern, a grand young fellow of eleven, with a reddish beard and a body like an athlete; and the inseparables, the blonde Helen Vance and the beautiful, laughing and arch-looking brunette Emma Vaughan. Full of health and happiness, and two of them wearers of the Magic Badge.

A railway line runs under the Grand Avenue to the Sea of Marmon, a distance of two hundred and fifty miles. This is the seaport of Sidonia. Our five friends went down by the morning express, and in two hours and a half they were on the shore of the second largest ocean on the planet. There is a great amount of traffic to this port, all the southern half of the city being supplied from it. The river Sidon, which cuts the city from its north-eastern corner diagonally, pours its clear flood into the ocean at this point.

For five hundred miles the Sidon is navigable for large vessels, and at that distance up and near to the Central Avenue there is an inland port, consisting of a pool two miles square and wharf accommodation for a score of great vessels. The whole course of the river from its mouth is never polluted. Ships going up are not allowed to discharge deck washings or any dirt into the river, and no sewage is permitted to flow into the river from any part. Ships, while on the river, in the pool, or at the wharves, are occupied as if they were houses on land, and their sewage has to be deodorised and desiccated day by day.

Our party took a launch driven by electric motors and propelled by a revolving keel, and Thomas Frankston made himself into sailing master and left the young people to their holiday and their freedom. It was decided that they should only travel by day. They wanted to see the country through its entire length, and to make the most of what they saw.

In one respect the river is a little monotonous in its lower portions. It is always clear and, though thirty feet in depth, the bottom is generally visible. Its banks, too, are grassed to the water's edge, except where a ferry boat crosses; that is every two miles or so. Railway tunnels run underneath at frequent intervals. Charlie Frankston told the party that the river was to a great extent a work of art. Through ages it had been dredged and widened. When the first Sidonia was built, a little village on the ocean shore, the river was a useless thing, emptying itself into the ocean through half a dozen shallow mouths. Sidonia grew and became a national capital and the Sidonians became a commercial and warlike nation. The Sea of Marmon was at last a Sidonian lake. Centuries of war and peace rolled on and the empire grew, and the Sidonian speech became the language of commerce. The world grew sick of war and the men of various nations entered into bonds of labour; they would not reduce the wages rate by underworking each other; they would not join military organisations to fight each other; they would work shorter hours and have some share of what they produced and made.

And it was time; for men had fought on land and on sea and had at length carried on battles in the air and a rain of blood had fallen upon the cities and the plains and bodies and mangled limbs had fallen into the streets.

Sidonia had become strong and rich and peaceful. She would not fight, but all the nations knew that her power and wealth would give her victory even if all the other nations were arrayed against her. Her power made for peace and she became the arbitrator of the nations. Her speech grew to be the language of the schools and the date line and the time ball were found in Sidonia. She grew into a sort of cosmopolitan capital – all men of mark had to drift towards her from all centres of population.

Still generations passed away and still Sidonia grew and grew. Within her boundaries the ambassadors of the nations met to discuss the terms of the Perpetual Peace and there they signed it. Sidonia then became a Federal Capital. The 'Black Century' came and taxed to the very uttermost the resources of the Sidonian Empire and the great Federation. In this time man grew to man, and each did what he could for the other; when this term was past all private fortunes were melted away. Meanwhile the Federal Council of ambassadors took upon itself the duties of the Central Executive and that body has been in existence ever since, always electing one from three selected ones when a member passed away or became unable to perform his or her arduous duties.

In song and story, in much friendly conversation, as well as in comparison of the old and new Sidonias, our party travels on. Love-making, too, is not wanting. Harry Hern seems to be successful and happy. Plainly Emma is little likely to return to her Antipodean home.

The Sabbath is spent in the River Port and all our party but Thomas Frankston, who is glad to excuse himself sometimes, spend part of the afternoon in the Central Avenue.

The next morning all are back on the river. They pass under the Central Avenue bridge, which divides the navigable from the ornamental parts of the river. Monotony ends here. From this point to its source the Sidon is a thing of beauty. A mile on each side is reserved as a public recreation ground for all time. The ground is broken and hilly and the landscape gardeners for centuries have been making the most of every advantage. There is no going up by the river. The launch has to be sent back from the first falls, which are wonderfully like the falls of Lodore about which a Martial Southey might have written in the same strain. Beetling crags, rockeries, islets, grottoes, ferneries, deep lagoons, riverside caves, deep pools, waterfalls, arches, funnels, shelters behind sheets of falling water … all, in short, that human ingenuity can design or conceive is there. Here and there models of machinery in motion are placed for the pleasure of the children.

For two weeks our party travelled through the Great Park of Sidonia, sometimes on one bank of the river, sometimes on the other, and their daily meal was sweetened by the sauce of appetite and their rest ensured by pleasant fatigue. No one was happier than Thomas Frankston. Daily he communicated with his dear wife and, watching his son and daughter, he felt his own youth renewed.

One day his Emma comes and strokes his hair and beard and plants herself on his knee and asks him if she has been guilty of neglect.

'No, my child, I have no blame for you on any count.'

'May I tell you something very serious, Father?' This time putting glowing face with red tingling shells of ears under her father's great brown beard.

'Yes, tell me what you will.'

'I am going to be married to Harry Hern.'

'Well,' said Thomas, 'I have no objection. Mother and I have known all about it for a long time, I will tell her this very hour.' Emma jumped up and ran away and in a few minutes Harry came to plead in person. His plea was granted.

Next day, they came to the boundary of the Great Park. It is the extreme north-eastern limit of Sidonia and at this point there is erected a triumphal arch a hundred feet in height. On one side are the words "Welcome to Sidonia". On the other side is written "Sidonia welcomes the river Sidon". Before it reaches this point, the Sidon does a vast amount of irrigation work. It was feared that there would be no river left. Instead of that it has been found that irrigation increases the river flow.

Further north is the sweet-water sea, but our party had spent three weeks in going from one part of the city to another and now they wanted to go home. They started back at thirteen o'clock by a local train to the north of Central Avenue. There they got the sixteen o'clock express that would land them at the Equatorial Hostel at twenty-one o'clock.

Thomas Frankston went to the reading room. Harry Hern and his beloved Emma might have been found sitting very near each other in a little conversational compartment. The five hours would not prove wearisome to them. Charles Frankston and Helen Vance were left to amuse each other.

'Well, Helen, we shall be home again in five hours. We cannot say that our pleasures will then be over, but this delightful time will be a memory.'

'For me a most pleasant one, Charlie. Kind friends, delightful weather and a constant succession of experiences all new and changeful.'

'I, too, Helen, look back on this as the very most enjoyable time of my life. And after all, the time spent in your company is the enjoyment. If you had remained at home all would have been spoiled.'

'There was never any serious danger of that. Emma could scarcely have gone so well if I had not been at liberty, and I will confess that I wished all the time to join the party.'

'You did?' said Charlie. 'Then possibly what animates me has perhaps some influence upon you. Oh, Helen, how often a question has trembled on my tongue, and I have not put it because you appeared so practical and friendly, so like a sister. I have feared to ask, lest the pleasant times we spend together should cease. I have feared again because there seemed to me some selfishness in asking you to devote your life to mine. I ask it now: can you love me? May we sweeten the cup of life for each other? Harry and Emma have set us the example, shall we follow them?'

Helen Vance again looked as she did when first she met Charlie on Mars. As for the strange vibration in her voice, that had never ceased. That far away look, that deep dumb something in the eye, what was it? Charlie could never see it without a quiver. There was some meaning for him in it.

'I would like to ask you a question or two, Charlie, about your Earth-life. Mine has been finished for three Earth-years, yours is not yet over. I have heard you say that you have a wife and children there. I left a husband and three sons in Melbourne.'

'But you have never told me much about your Earth-life, and when I have tried to lead up to the subject you have always turned from it. You never even said so much as you have just told me. Never mentioned Melbourne, to which city Grayson took me for half an hour long since. We have dwelt in the same city. We may have seen and known each other. From our first meeting I have felt as if we had some memory in common. Indeed, that feeling has always had a strong hold upon me: you have always made me wish to remember.'

'Your missing memory is coming, coming fast,' said Helen. 'It is almost time that you knew as much as I have known from the first. What sort of woman was your Earth-wife when you saw her in the state induced by Grayson?'

'She was a robust woman of nearly sixty years of age, wife-like and motherly. I felt when I saw her as if I were at once a grandson and a husband to her. Her voice was deep and full, and had a verve in it.'

Here Charlie paused as if forced into silence and sat swaying to and fro as if only partly conscious. He put his face between his hands and bowed himself forward. Helen watched him with every faculty upon the stretch. Again he looked up into the face of Helen Vance, and continued.

'It was your voice, and the eyes. With the wrinkled forehead and the crown of gray hair above them were your eyes. You, *you*, YOU are the same. My loved wife for forty years, the same! The *same*!! The SAME!!! Thank God we meet again.'

Charlie rose from his seat in his emotion and tried to clasp Helen in his arms. In doing so he staggered from side to side and then fell. The rush of consciousness had suspended animation. A moment more and his father, Harry, and Emma were there, and the unconscious man was made comfortable while the train rushed on to Sidonia.

In two hours he was in Grayson's house and Doctor Somers was in attendance upon him.

CHAPTER XVII

A Marriage

'H ELEN.'

'Yes, Charlie.'

Charlie sat up and looked round him. 'How long have I been here?'

'Just one day, Charlie,' replied Helen. 'You fell in the carriage, you know, and we brought you to Grayson's to recover. Hearing what had happened, Doctor Somers came at once and sent for Felix Henderson, the great alienist. They consulted over your case and came to the conclusion that you would awaken soon and be well. They left me with you, and Grayson is within call. They said we would be able to help you to put your mind in order, as our experiences were in some senses similar.'

'I do not feel anything wrong now,' said Charlie. 'I know I am living two lives, but they are not mixed. While I have been lying here I have been getting a full knowledge of my Earth-life and history. We have now subjects of conversation in common. If our life here does not provide us with enough to think about we can speak about our previous life. The lonely half of me that is working down there will be happier now that my consciousness of his life is established. There is nothing now to hinder us from marrying and living a still happier life than the last.'

'Oh, yes, there is. We have not been betrothed; I have not promised to marry you.'

'Now, Helen, don't tease. You know that we two have to marry and you have known it for years.'

'Nonsense. Our having been married for forty years does not of necessity involve marrying again. You might have found someone else and so might I. What if you had not crossed the snow that night? What if you had found me half an hour later?'

'True, but I did find you and we have loved each other with a new love irrespective of the old one. Indeed, it is just possible that the same couple might be married in both planets and in each know nothing about the marriage in the other.'

'We'll let that subject drop for the present,' said Helen. 'I will go and tell Doctor Somers that you have no further need of her aid, and you will see Grayson directly.'

Charlie spent an hour with Grayson that afternoon and received the congratulations of many of his friends on having so easily got through his crisis. The Earthborns especially welcomed him as now capable of bringing his quota of news from the lower sphere.

Three days later there was a very pleasing ceremony in Frankston's rooms at the Equatorial. It was the marriage of Emma Vaughan and Harry Hern. The four members of the Frankston family, the three of the Hern family, and the Teacher who officiated at the cremation of Thomas Hern were present, together with Grayson, his wife, and a few select friends of the young people.

In the middle of the room a small dais was placed, and on this two chairs. Charlie Frankston led Harry Hern to one of these seats and his mother led her daughter Emma to the other. The Teacher then stood up, and facing the little group upon and around the dais, said or read:

'We meet this afternoon to solemnise the marriage of our dear young friends Emma Vaughan and Harry Hern. They are well assured that they love each other with a pure and strong affection, a love that will last through life and that cannot be destroyed. Such a love is the best if not the only reason for marrying; without it there can be no true marriage, no happy family life. Such a love is sacred. It leads to the founding and sustaining of the family and to the moral purity of social life. This in turn reacts upon every phase of life and marks us as a virtuous and happy people. In uniting these two in the bonds of conjugal affection we lay the foundation of another happy home. We do something more towards promoting the social order which has been a leading feature of our life for ages and we add to the sum total of the enjoyment of life. Our young friends will now rise and clasp hands, saying, "We two love each other with an enduring conjugal affection, a love that causes each to seek to benefit the other, even at the expense of self-sacrifice. Our desire is to dwell together for life, to work together for the common good, to participate in each other's labours and enjoyments, to have interests in common, to worship together, to share joys and sorrows, to be true and helpful to each other in prosperity or adversity. We each endow the other with the wealth of love we can bestow and we go through life side by side as comrades and equals. From you, Teacher and Pastor, we ask the benediction of the church, and from our parents, relatives and friends, a continuation of the love and sympathy they have ever shown towards us.'"

The Pastor then stepped forward, and raising his hands over the now kneeling pair, said, 'May the Divine blessing rest upon these two, whom I now declare to be man and wife, until the expiration of their present term of life, Amen.'

And all answered, 'Amen.'

In the afternoon, the marriage was registered in the district registry. The newly married pair remained in the metropolis for another week and then went with Mother Vance to their home in Highton. The three families arranged to spend thirty days of each year in each other's company, the Badges of Freedom assisting materially.

Charlie had been many times to the Observatory and had learned to use the giant telescopes, both the reflector and the refractor. He had made arrangements, too, with the Astronomer-in-Chief, to be present. Doctor Mark Haley was there to meet the rather numerous party, and Grayson, with one of his sons, came early in the morning. About twenty-three o'clock, Charlie and one of Haley's juniors commenced a general sweeping of the heavens with the refractor. They studied double stars, decomposed nebula, showed the rings of Saturn to be composed of millions of little globes moving at varying rates and never clashing with each other; they saw the moons of Uranus, four of them being in sight; studied the surface of that cold, faraway planet, and found that there were unmistakable signs of habitation by beings doubtless adapted to it.

Nearly three hours passed away as if they had been but moments. One little incident caused some momentary alarm and amusement. Harry Hern was at the eyepiece of the telescope, one hand on Emma's shoulder, she having just stepped aside. For a moment he looked steadily and then jumped back in fright, his eyes staring widely and his hair actually bristling.

'Oh! Oh!!' he cried. 'A great orb is falling upon us.'

He seized Emma and started to run away, as if that could do any good. The junior astronomer caught him and bid him look again. There, all was as before, the red and blue stars scintillating in the silent heavens.

'What was it?' asked Harry.

'It was our nearest moon. It is so near that it always appears as if falling upon the larger telescopes.'

Harry was teased for many a day for his attempt to run away with Emma. As for his start, that was pardonable.

CHAPTER XVIII

A Betrothal. Conclusion

DOCTOR MARK HALEY and his junior had now gone to the great reflector. For a short time the Earth would be in a favourable position for observation. When nearest to Mars it is out of sight and has its dark side turned that way. From the Earth, Mars is then a full-face study, and sometimes only forty millions of miles distant. Seen from Mars, however, the Earth is only full when at its greatest distance. This night the Earth was half full, and Australia would emerge into the sunlight about one o'clock, Martial time. The great reflector, and all connected with it, are moved back by clockwork just as fast as Mars moves forward on its axis, so that the Earth, now in the field of vision, shall remain fixed there, presenting only such changes as result from its own motion. All the party had a peep at the illuminated half of the Earth, which in the mighty speculum appeared as half a sphere of twenty inches in diameter. Several now left. Harry, Grayson, his son, and Charlie and Helen remained. Two sat at one side, three at the other, the great pit of the instrument separating them.

The sun shone brightly over the North and South Pacific. North America was wrapped in fogs and clouds. It was summer in the Southern Seas. A little speck came into sight and was instantly identified as New Caledonia. Two larger ones further south were known as New Zealand. A few minutes more and the Queensland coast of the Australian continent merges into the sunlight. Running the eye south over its broken and indented edge, Helen and Charlie simultaneously saw Port Jackson.

'Our first home was there, Helen,' said Charlie, with emotion.

'True, we spent many happy years there,' replied Helen. 'How much more pleasant life might have been if we had not followed the gold and tried to become rich.'

'There is Port Phillip and that black spot in the northern corner is Melbourne, where now my first identity glances up at the coming day and lies wearily back for another nap. Poor man, he has long been a widower and his work is hard. Would not you like to comfort him, Helen, as of yore?'

'I will.' And she put her hand on Charlie's forehead.

A moment later the old man looked round and said, 'How pleasant. A moment ago I was young again and felt the caressing touch of my dear wife.'

Of this both Charlie and Helen were conscious.

The sun now shone upon half the continent and lit up Japan and Eastern China, and bathed the Indian Islands in its light. Charles put his arm round Helen's waist and said, 'Now, Helen, tell me, when shall we renew the holy compact which we both so faithfully kept for forty years in the toil and turmoil of yonder grand but yet only half-developed world?'

'Look at Melbourne again,' said Helen.

'I am looking.'

'See you a small green space, a mere pin point, to the north of the City?' asked Charlie's questioner.

'I see it, and know what it is.'

'In a short time that weary old man, the Earth half of you who is now preparing for the labours of another day, will lay down his earthly covering and you will be all here. In two more days that pin speck of green will receive the mortal remains of Adam Jacobs, my widowed husband. While your kin and friends follow that shell to its resting place, and mourn your decease, we will solemnise our marriage in the most appropriate place, the Great Hall of the Earthborn's Club. Now the day is fixed, Charlie dear.'

'I agree,' said Charlie. 'It is well. We'll tell Grayson.'

The Editor could not mourn when, the other day, he read of the decease of Jacobs, nor could he record the marriage at the club, for the hand of the diarist could pen no more of the bright pages on which we have dwelt so long.

THE END

GRATTAN STREET PRESS PERSONNEL

Semester 1, 2020

Editing and Proofreading
Elizabeth Adams – Lead Copyeditor and Proofreader
Paulina Hernandez – Copyeditor
Bahar Kutluk – Copyeditor and Proofreader
Maddison Moore – Proofreader
Greer Sutherland – Chief Proofreader

Design and Production
Greer Sutherland – Production Editor

Sales and Marketing
Farzeen Imtiaz – Sales Manager
Joseph Carbone – Sales Officer
Paulina Hernandez – Publicity Co-ordinator

Social Media
Joseph Carbone – Social Media Manager
Farzeen Imtiaz – Social Media Officer

Submissions Officers
Maddison Moore – Commissioning Editor

Website and Blogs
Monique Courtney – Website Producer and Manager
Bahar Kutluk – Blog Editor

Academic Staff
Sybil Nolan and Katherine Day

ACKNOWLEDGEMENTS

This semester's Colonial Australian Popular Fiction offering would not have been possible without the engagement of our volume editors: Alexandra Roginski and Zachary Kendal. We thank them for sharing their enthusiasm and passion for this progressive and fascinating text, as well as some valuable insights into the story and its eccentric author.

Publishing a book in a short period of time requires a high level of commitment and focus. Considering that *Melbourne and Mars* was produced during a pandemic, with new modes of learning and skills to navigate online, this semester's GSP cohort have been tremendous. Many thanks to the dedicated editorial and production teams: Elizabeth Adams, Paulina Hernandez, Bahar Kutluk, Maddison Moore and Greer Sutherland. The concerted efforts of our sales and marketing and publicity teams ensured that we were able to share this title with its audience. Thanks to Joseph Carbone, Monique Courtney, Paulina Hernandez and Farzeen Imtiaz for their research into how to publicise a book in a global lockdown, and their adaptability.

Thank you to Mark Davis, who designed the series cover and internal text and advised the students; and thanks also to Ken Gelder and Rachael Weaver for their continuing support for the Press, and for providing us with wonderful texts to publish. Their generosity and knowledge are instrumental to the success of this series. We are also very grateful for the help of our Head of School, Peter Otto.

Finally, thanks to Debbie Lee, Rushelle Lister and all of the staff at our printer, IngramSpark.

Katherine Day, Managing Editor, Grattan Street Press

ABOUT THE AUSTRALIAN CENTRE

The Australian Centre is based in the School of Culture and Communication at the University of Melbourne, with Professor Ken Gelder and Professor Denise Varney as its co-directors. It aims to develop innovative research projects in the Australian arts and humanities across a wide range of disciplines, including Art History, Theatre Studies, Literary Studies, Cultural Studies, Media and Communications, Cinema Studies, Indigenous studies and Creative Writing.

ABOUT GRATTAN STREET PRESS

Grattan Street Press is a trade publisher based in Melbourne. A start-up press, we aim to publish a range of work, including contemporary literature and trade non-fiction, and re-publish culturally valuable works that are out of print. The press is an initiative of the Publishing and Communications program in the School of Culture and Communication at the University of Melbourne, and is staffed by graduate students, who receive hands-on experience of every aspect of the publication process.

The press is a not-for-profit organisation that seeks to build long-term relationships with the Australian literary and publishing community. We also partner with community organisations in Melbourne and beyond to co-publish books that contribute to public knowledge and discussion.

Organisations interested in partnering with us can contact us at coordinator@grattanstreetpress.com. Writers interested in submitting a manuscript to Grattan Street Press can contact us at editorial@grattanstreetpress.com.